DISOBEDIENT BRIDE

A DARK ANGEL ROMANCE

LOKI RENARD

1

E *lise*

Someone is in my apartment.

I hear them moving around in the kitchen, and then I hear footsteps coming toward the bedroom. The clock tells me it is three minutes past three in the morning. Nobody should be here. My lips part to call out to ask who it is, but there is an older kind of fear that stops me from making any noise. I am frozen, my fingers clutching the coverlet, my breath short and shallow.

The steps are drawing closer. Closer. I want to believe this is a nightmare, but I am wide awake and completely helpless.

The door to my bedroom opens, and a man I have never met or seen before enters. He's not wearing a face covering, and I can see his features cast in the light from the lounge. He has turned all the lights on, and now he flicks my bedroom light on too.

He is tall and he is broad and he has a sort of vicious expression on his face that would frighten me even if he wasn't in my bedroom at three in the morning. Worse still, he is holding a knife. Not a kitchen knife. Not a machete. It is a thin rapier-type knife, a ceremonial blade which I am certain is just as sharp as any other.

He comes toward me without speaking. I have managed to get out of bed, but I would have to go past him to escape, and that is not going to happen.

I scream for help, but I know none will come. There's no hope. My neighbors are old and deaf. I chose this building because it was quiet, not because it had good security. I never thought anything like this would happen to me. I'm not a flashy sort of girl. I'm the kind nobody notices. So I never expected to be noticed. I certainly never expected to be accosted by a knife-wielding maniac in my own home.

He grabs me, and the world goes into slow motion. I feel the vise-like grip of his massive hand on my wrist, spinning me around back toward the bed. Everything is so slow, but I don't have time to think. All I can do is watch as my life is taken away. He releases my wrist and lunges for my neck. He is trying to pin me down by my throat. He doesn't just want to stab me. He wants to stab me in a very specific way.

I am fighting him with everything I have. He's much stronger, but I am battling for my life and that means I am using every bit of my strength to do that, even the parts you don't usually have access to, desperate reserves of power drawn from every one of my cells.

It's not enough to stop him.

The tip of the knife scratches my arm, biting deep. Blood starts to flow, and my panic rises. He's going to kill me, and there's nothing I can do.

"Stop wasting the blood!"

He speaks for the first time in a predictably accented voice, and the order is terrifying. It's not enough that he stabbed me. He also seems inconvenienced by the way I am bleeding. He wants me to be more orderly about it, stereotypically German.

"Hey! Asshole!"

Suddenly there's a second man in my apartment. This one has an American accent. There has never been one man in my apartment before, and now there are two. My attacker turns his head just in time to receive tattooed knuckles directly to his jaw. There's a crunch as his neck snaps backward and the rest of his body follows inexorably.

The American has blue hair and the expression of someone who is very much enjoying what he is doing, which is beating the hell out of my attacker. His muscular arms are pumping back and forth with harsh blows, hands like tattooed hammers inflicting massive damage on the face and body of my assailant.

I crawl back against the wall, knees to my chest, watching in horror as the violence unfolds before me. The German has dropped the knife and is trying to defend himself, but whoever the American man is with the dark and narrowed eyes, clenched jaw, and general air of aggressive menace, he's not stopping.

The German tries to counterattack, but he's on his back on the ground under a hail of fists that turn into a grabbing grapple of some kind as the American decides to finish matters by grabbing the knife and...

I close my eyes. I can't watch. I think I might be screaming. Am I screaming? I can't hear myself. Everything sounds like blood and ringing in my ears.

I am picked up in very large arms and carried out of the bedroom, away from what my gut tells me is now a body.

"It's okay," the man who just killed someone in my bedroom says. "You're safe, angel."

I am frozen in place as he sets me up on the kitchen counter. Safe? I am not safe.

I feel his fingers beneath my chin. "Look at me," he orders softly but firmly.

I open my eyes to look at him and find myself staring into a face of such perfect, handsome brutality I feel a pang in my gut, a kind of pain of yearning that comes with seeing someone so fucking far out of my league it's like we're not even the same classification of creature.

He's putting pressure on the cut on my arm. "Can you lift that up? Good girl," he praises as I raise my arm. "It's not so bad."

I barely even notice the wound. I am too busy staring at him. He has deep blue hair, almost black, and very handsome dark narrow eyes, like those of a hunter. The lines of his face are fine and yet masculine. He could be a back-alley mugger or a model in a fashion magazine. He's of mixed heritage, a sort of rougher, bulkier Neo breaking into my Matrix.

He's covered in tattoos, the exposed parts of his hands and up his neck almost to his jaw. He's dangerous, and he's violent, but fortunately he knows how to bandage a stab wound with great alacrity. He's grinning as he works, almost as if he enjoys this. I watch him with a dazed and disembodied feeling, like this isn't really happening. Like I'm still asleep.

"You're going to be okay, angel. Lucky I got here in time..."

"Who are you?"

"My name is Cosmos," he tells me.

"That's not a name."

"It's the name my mama gave me," he replies. Can't argue with that. A mama's right to name her child is absolute.

"Thank you, Cosmos," I say. "I don't know who that was..."

"Of course not," he says. "You're an innocent angel."

There's something about the way he uses the word "angel" that is making it sound less like a soothing term of casual affection and more like... something else.

"My name's Elise."

"Uh huh. I know."

"How do you know?"

He looks me deep in my eyes. "Elise, that man came to kill you. He won't be the only one. You need to come with me. Now."

"Why would anybody come for me? We should go to the police."

"The police can't help with this," he says. "If there is anything in this place you can't live without, now is the time to get it. We will not be coming back here."

"What do you mean we're not coming back?"

"Anything of sentimental value. Anything handed down to you. Anything you'd spend the rest of your life regretting having left behind. Take it now."

"But..."

"NOW!"

He shouts the word, startling me. I don't know what I need. I have never had to consider what I'd take with me if I had to leave my life in a matter of minutes. And I don't want to go back into my bedroom, because that's where the body is, and...

I burst into tears. I don't know what's happening and being yelled at by a massive, murderous man is more than I can take after everything else.

"Christ," he murmurs under his breath, taking me by the shoulders. "Okay. Look at me. Passport. Family photos. Anything belonging to a grandparent. Animal mementos. Clothes. Do you have a bag here somewhere?"

"In the closet," I blubber.

"Okay. Is this it?" He goes to the closet and pulls out my day bag. It's a cute pink little suitcase on wheels with an extendable handle. In his grip, it looks ludicrous.

"Yes."

"Alright, Elise. You've got to work with me here. Let's get your documents together, something to wear, come on. You can do it. Good girl."

I respond to good girl much better than I do angel. I find myself obeying him because I don't have enough bandwidth to do anything else. My home has been invaded. My life has been threatened, and this mysterious, violent stranger is taking control.

I'm not even entirely sure what I'm taking, I just know that I'm doing what I'm told, and that's easier than trying to make a decision based on my own experiences, which are basically nil.

"Let's go," he repeats when the bag is full. He grips me by the arm and leads me out of my apartment down to the front of the building where a van is idling. Of course it is a van. Men like him don't drive cars. They need more storage for... horrors, I suppose.

He helps me into the passenger seat, and then slings my bag into the dark void at the back. I hold my arm where I have been stabbed. It's starting to ache. I'm starting to feel, even though that's probably a mistake. I sit there while he walks around to the driver's side. He passes the front of the van, and the light from the street lamps gleams off his blue hair. God. I've never seen anybody like him before.

Cosmos gets in beside me and glances over at me. "Put your seatbelt on."

I can't put my seatbelt on. The wound on my arm makes it hard to reach across. Cosmos realizes this at the same time I do. He leans over me. I feel his hard body brushing against mine. He smells like expensive cologne. Why didn't I notice that before? Too panicked, perhaps. He snaps my seatbelt into place and gives me a wink.

From abject terror to a sense of safety, I have swung wildly from one emotional state to another over the course of the last hour. It has left me not only wounded, but exhausted.

We drive into the darkness of Heidelberg, the city I adopted several years ago. It is a city of old ruins and great history. It is also where my laboratory is situated.

"What just happened? Who was that?"

He glances over at me. "I will explain soon."

He's pulling up outside a church. I am confused. A hospital would seem more appropriate. I'm already getting the idea that nothing Cosmos does is appropriate.

"They won't follow us here," he explains, helping me out of the van. "There are friends inside. Let's go."

He has an urgency and a momentum to him that is very captivating. I am not used to being around men like him. The men in the lab are like me, logical and mostly dedicated to work. I was dating one of them, but not in an intense, passionate way. More in a, well, we're going to need someone to settle down with eventually, sort of way. It was a passionless affair. We never even got around to having sex.

Cosmos escorts me from the van and up the steps of the old church. It feels solid and safe. Candlelight flickers inside and there are several hooded figures apparently waiting for us.

Cosmos leads me toward the altar. I suddenly realize I am still in my Hello Bunny nightgown. It is pink with little white bunnies on it. Some of them have been spattered with blood. My blood. It has dried in little speckles over their cute noses. I am a mess. I need a shower and I need to be properly dressed and I need to speak to the authorities.

"What is her name?" the priest at the altar asks.

"Let's call her Bunny," Cosmos says.

"Welcome, Cosmos and Bunny," the priest says after a moment. He leans toward Cosmos. "You will need to use your legal names for the license."

"Yes. I know. Just carry on. We don't have much time."

I stare at him, not knowing what the hell he is talking about. Now that we are standing together, he is much taller than me. He's literally larger than life, a big beast emerged from the darkness to claim me. I am in survival mode, dazed, confused, and not entirely sure any of this is real.

The priest begins to speak.

"Marriage is the promise of..."

Cosmos makes a winding motion with his right index finger. "We don't really have times for the bells and whistles, Father. Let's do this."

"Do you, Cosmos, take Bunny to be your wife?"

"I do," he says.

What the everloving fuck is going on?

"Do you, Bunny, take Cosmos to be your husband?"

I open my mouth, not knowing what to say.

"I do…"

Cosmos cuts me off before I can finish the sentence, which was going to be *I don't know what's happening.*

"There we go!" he says, clapping his hand over my mouth. "She said I do. It counts! We're done!"

"In the eyes of God, I pronounce you man and wife," the priest says. "You may now consummate the marriage."

Wait. What? Isn't the line supposed to be you may now kiss the bride? Consummate? Isn't that… that's sex. I stare up at this tall, brutally handsome man and I feel twin chills of fear and excitement at the possibility of sleeping with him.

"Don't worry," he says. "I won't hurt you. But we have to make this real. There's a room in the back."

He sweeps me up into his arms, the way grooms traditionally do when preparing to carry their new brides over the threshold of their new home. Instead of a new home, I am carried into a lavish, red velvet covered room with a bed in it. What kind of church is this, exactly?

I never imagined my wedding night would be a wedding morning, and that my dress would be blood-spattered pajamas. It all feels surreal. Everything except the strong, muscular arms wrapped around me. They're very real, very hot, and very strong.

Cosmos lays me down tenderly on red velvet and looks down at me with lust-hooded eyes.

"Are you a virgin?"

Cosmos

She looks like a deer caught in headlights, poor thing. I take a handkerchief from a pocket and use it to dab some of the blood from her cheek.

"I can't..."

"Why not? Do you have another partner?" Even saying the words makes me burn with jealousy. I already feel incredibly possessive of this angel blood girl. I sought her out. I saved her in the nick of time. She's mine, and I want to feel the soft, hot parts of her. I want to claim her and make her know in her soul who she belongs to. The ceremony was for God. The sex is for us.

"No. I don't have a partner."

I take my place next to her, still dressed, but intimately close. So close I can feel her trembling against me. She's scared. Is it residual terror from her attacker? Or am I just as terrifying?

"Do you want to be fucked by me, Elise? Have you wondered what it would be like to be with someone like me?"

"Someone like you?" She pretends to be confused, but I can see the light in her pretty eyes. She knows exactly what I mean. Someone rough, someone dangerous, a man who knows what he wants and takes it. Someone who calls fucking, fucking.

"This has been a very bad night for you so far," I tell her. "But it could be the best night of your life."

I drop my head, cup her chin, and kiss her. Her kiss is hesitant at first, but soon flowers into hot desire. I knew it. Her cool, almost frigid exterior is melting for me already. I taste the fire inside her as I stoke embers long left to smolder.

Elise

What am I doing? Why am I allowing this? A thousand thoughts race through my mind and are promptly scattered by the feeling of his hard body pressing against mine, his cock throbbing against my belly through our clothes.

I am a virgin.

I am a virgin because I judge men ruthlessly and find most of them to be utterly intolerable. I am turned off by stupidity and laziness and arrogance, and I cannot be bothered to cater to the fragile ego of someone who does not understand my life was and always will be fully complete without him.

Cosmos' kiss eradicates all thought. He is a physical creature, an animal. I don't know if he can truly be considered a man. He is too urgent, impulsive, and instinctive to be fully human, surely.

His large hands cup my ass and snug me close, drawing my sex harder against his cock through our clothes — his black tactical pants and my blood-spattered, not-at-all tactical bunnies. This is already more filthy and intimate than any encounter in my life.

He is making me feel like the most elegant bride, the most desired creature in all the universe. I never understood what people meant before when they talked about *chemistry*. I would get annoyed with them for misusing scientific terms for sociological relationships. I feel it now. I feel the crackle of desire sparking across synapses, and the charge of hormones and pheromones. I am experiencing a truly chemical reaction to him.

I'm going to let this happen.

That thought comes to me and I accept it as truth. Yes, I am going to be with this man. I don't know him, and he has tricked me into marriage, but there is nothing fake about the way my clit is tingling and pulsing in answer to the grinding of his cock.

"You're such a dirty little thing," he purrs softly. He's referring to my clothing, I think, but he is also making full use of the double entendre. His hands are on my shoulders as he begins to strip my messy clothes from me, leaving me naked. He is still clothed, and I feel the imbalance of power instantly. It is fucking hot.

"Beautiful," he breathes, complimenting me. I find myself blushing not just because of my nudity, but because he is so entranced by me. I am sure he has slept with many beautiful women before. He has the looks and confidence to have ladies dropping at his feet. His fixation with me feels very odd. I am not accustomed to being desired in this openly carnal way. Yes, men ask me out from time to time, but I never agree. I have my work to satisfy me.

My work... thoughts of it are cut off again as he kisses me once more and lays me back on a velvet coverlet. I feel the rich fabric soft against my skin, the candlelight flickering across my body, casting me in romantic light.

He strips off his own clothing now, baring a tattooed chest, over which a baroque demon and angel are drawn locked in struggle. He is like a walking Sistine Chapel, full of true art. I could stare at it for hours — until he pushes his pants down and his cock emerges, long and thick and hard.

"What the..." I gasp, clasping my hand to my mouth.

"Have you not seen a penis before?" He asks the question with a gratified chuckle. He is sexy as hell when he smirks, standing in front of me muscular and ready to take me. His tattoos mean he's not really naked so much as he is ink-clad.

Yes, I have seen a penis before. Just not in real life, and not with this much intimate intention for my own body. The thick head of his cock bobs toward me, almost as if it has a mind of its own.

"You are a virgin," he says, reading me like a book even though I have not a line of text on me. I am so obvious to him, and that makes me blush more furiously than ever.

"Don't hide your eyes from me," he adds when I look away from him. "This is destiny. Do you not feel the hand of fate on you? You've preserved your innocence up until this moment, and now we will bond, my sweet bride."

He's a stranger, but he is a stranger who makes my blood heat with that infernal desire I can barely contain. I have gone from being terrified in the place I should have felt safest, to wildly aroused in the place I should feel afraid.

I'm not the kind to sleep with strangers, but this man has a dark hold on me. He creates a certain fascination that demands to be sated. I can feel my body preparing for him, wetness growing between my thighs, and a hot, tingling anticipation making my thighs spread. I am not the sort of person to let go and give into instinct, but some biological urges are too intense to avoid.

He covers my body with his own, his muscular arms on either side of me as he holds himself above me, keeping the bulk of his weight off me as he kisses me again. These hot kisses are maddening, like little doses of a drug that can only be fully delivered by his cock. My hips rise toward him, and I feel his cock pressing against my pubic bone. I did not know it would be that hot. When I arch my hips, I tilt my pelvis and make my clit press against his thick rod.

Words escape us now, fleeing as unnecessary little sounds that will not change a thing. I am wrapped in his embrace, caressed by his marked hands. I am explored by his lips and tongue. He finds my breasts and toys with them, his tongue teasing my nipples into harder, higher points. I am surprised by how his mouth at my breast sends intense bolts of sensation to join the rest of my arousal. He is working me up to a sexual frenzy, tapping into a hidden vein of carnal need. I've always told myself I don't need a man, or his cock. My vibrator has always been more than enough.

But a vibrator doesn't pin me down and kiss me with ever rougher intensity, it doesn't set all my senses alight and make my imagination race with desire. I want him inside me. I want to know what it feels like to be stretched around this dark, beautiful stranger's cock.

He is not in any hurry to claim me. He could have speared himself inside me by now, but he is taking his time. He is showing me a myriad of sexual features I did not know were locked away behind my skin. I find myself relaxing, spreading, giving myself to him like a submissive sacrifice. Some part of my mind thinks I will wake up in my bed again, that this is just a vivid dream. A better, more knowing part of my mind knows that this is destiny. I like to think that I determine my future through my actions, but at times like these I can feel the strings of biology making me little more than a puppet. I am as compelled to take my rescuer's thick cock as I am to breathe.

"Are you ready for me, my sweet virgin bride?" He growls the question down at me, simultaneously flexing the length of his body, lifting himself up a little higher, his arms imprisoning me against the bed, his cock sliding from the down of my sex where it had been nestled to press against the wet entrance of my body. The thick head of his cock is now poised to claim me, my outer lips already wrapped about the hot, throbbing glans.

I gasp in a breath and nod, but that is not enough consent for him. He demands more. He wants to hear me tell him to tear my virginity away, to claim a part of me no man has ever had before.

"Please," I whimper.

"You ask so nicely," he praises. "What a very good girl."

With each of those words, he lets his hips sink down toward the core of me, his weight pushing the head of his cock inside me. I feel myself stretch. At first it feels fine, but a moment later there is a hot, searing feeling. I draw my legs up alongside his hips and let out a whimper. He stills immediately, brushing strands of hair away from my flushed face.

"It's okay," he assures me. "Breathe."

I let out the breath I didn't know I was holding and my pussy relaxes. The intensity of the tight sting inside me fades and in its place comes a feeling of fullness. Cosmos sinks himself deeper. Deeper. He moves slowly until he is as far inside me as anybody might be able to go. I feel myself stretched and claimed. I feel myself throbbing in time with his cock. For a long moment, he keeps himself there, sheathed deep inside me. I remember him saying this was all he really needed to do. The joining of the flesh. Is this it?

He begins to pull back and it is all I can do to stop myself from trying to grab his muscular ass with my hands to hold him inside me. I don't want him to leave me. I don't want this feeling to stop. I whine as his cock nearly exits completely — and then he surges deep inside again.

Cosmos starts to stroke inside me, and I lose my mind. It feels so good. It feels so, so fucking good, all I can do is whimper those words over and over again.

C osmos

This hot little virgin is writhing on my cock, cursing up a storm.

"Fuck, fuck, yes fuck, please fuck yes..."

Her near constant stream of carnal begging is so sweet. Her cunt is gripping me with the same desperation I see in her eyes and hear in her voice. She doesn't know what is coming, but I think she feels it, an orgasm building in her body as she starts to shake and tremble around me. She's going to go off soon, and that is good because this tight, wet, virgin cunt is perilously close to making me come.

There is something so fucking intense about being with her. From the moment she laid down before me and spread her thighs with that innocent willingness I was on the verge of spilling myself. It's not usually a problem I have. Stamina is my forte, but this woman, my bride, she demands my seed deep inside her.

I will not disappoint her. I take both her wrists in one hand and hold them up above her head. I suspect she will like the feeling of being held, and the way her cunt grips me even tighter proves my suspicions correct as I unleash a fraction of my strength, fucking her with powerful, commanding strokes. Next time I take her, I will pound this hot cunt. This time I will keep myself in check, fucking her virginity from her with practiced, controlled thrusts which turn her quivering and writhing and begging into full blown squeals of climax. She grips me tight both with her pussy and with her soft hands, her legs wrapped around my thighs as she milks me. Her body is not just experiencing orgasm, it is demanding my own accompany it.

Who am I to disappoint a lady? I let go. I release my seed with a roar, slamming inside her, pinning her down and filling her tightness with my come. Yes. Yes. Yes, fucking yes. My little angel is absolutely mine.

Elise

I've never felt this way before. I've never felt so completely relaxed and so totally taken. The orgasm I just had with Cosmos inside me was more powerful than anything I have ever experienced sexually. I feel as though every single cell of my body has been depleted of a little energy, but in the best way.

He's still inside, his cock pulsing and throbbing as the final spurts of his masculine essence defile what's left of my virginity.

"You are so fucking..." He kisses me deeply before finishing his sentence. "Perfect."

I feel all warm and cozy and... as he pulls out, I feel something hot gush from me. It takes me far too long to realize what that wet heat is. It is his cum. His seed. He just fucking came in me.

I reach down between my legs and feel the wetness, lifting my fingers up to find them coated in a cloudy, sticky, milky mix.

I look up at him with wide eyes. "What did you do..."

"I made you mine," he smiles, so tenderly I find it hard to be mad at him. I knew he wasn't wearing a condom. I didn't tell him not to come in me. I didn't say anything. I laid back and let him fuck me, and now I am absolutely brimming with virile seed.

"You made a baby. Idiot."

"I absolutely did not, moron."

I burst out laughing, mostly in shock. "What!?"

"I had a vasectomy as soon as I could. My line of work does not provide any time for rearing offspring. The Brotherhood retires any of its members who have children."

"And if I wanted children?"

"Your single lifestyle and virginity suggest they might not be a priority."

"Or I was saving myself for marriage, to then bear fruit."

He looks uncomfortable as I quote bible-ish stuff at him.

"That might be something we discuss later," he says.

"Just kidding. Look at your face!" I laugh. I don't want kids. I can barely handle myself most of the time and being a career driven woman means knowing full well I won't be given any promotions in my company if I go off and get pregnant. I've never really seriously considered a relationship, let alone a baby.

"Come," Cosmos says, handing me my filthy clothes. "We need to get out of here."

I do not want to put them on again, but I also don't want to be taken out of here naked and dripping his seed, and I have a feeling that would very much be on his agenda if he could put it on the agenda. He's a twisted soul in a beautiful body — and I just gave myself to him.

2

I am dressed again, such as you can consider this dressed. My discomfort putting my clothing on must be obvious.

"We can change your clothes at our next stop," Cosmos says. "And have a shower. Don't worry. Everything is going to be okay."

I have to trust him, because not trusting him means I just let someone I don't know, or trust, take me through a marriage ceremony and take my virginity besides. This has been a night of madness, and I don't know how I will ever become sane again.

I am sensible enough to know this is not how marriage works. You can't trick someone into saying I do in front of a priest and call that a wedding. There's paperwork to be done, there are forms to be signed, and...

I let out a squeal as Cosmos sweeps me up into his arms. He carries me out of our dark love chamber, back down the aisle, and tucks me back into the van.

"Lucky we got that done," he says, putting my seatbelt on again. "That could have been dangerous."

He's referring to having gotten my virginity done. Or maybe the 'marriage,' such as it was. With the cool night air and the return to the less than comfortable van, sense is beginning to return. The post-coital afterglow is fading, and I realize that I just don't understand what's happening, at all.

"What is happening?" Those three words cover a multitude of questions.

"Well, dear wife, what is happening is I just saved you from an ancient Germanic cult of blood hunters who seek the angel blood that runs in your veins."

He's delusional. I've been kidnapped by a madman. I'd think he was a complete and utter liar if not for the fact I am still bleeding from the attacker who turned my world upside down not long ago.

I stare at him, wondering if I am mad too, or if it was just the trauma and relief of surviving the brutal attack that made me submit to his desire and impulsively give him the one thing I saved for so long.

In the distance, the sun is starting to rise. Reality asserts itself with the golden glow over Heidelberg Palace. I remember that I have a life, a real life, and real responsibilities. I can't sit around in my pajamas bleeding in vans. I have to go and decant the samples I prepared yesterday.

"I'm going to be late for work!"

"You're not going to go to work," he says gently. "I'm taking you back to England, where I can continue to safeguard you. Your marriage to me makes you safer, but there are some who do not respect the bounds of holy matrimony."

I look at him, this rakish madman, and I attempt to formulate some set of words that might make him realize how crazy this all really is.

"Okay. Well. First. There are no such things as angels, or demons," I explain in the calmest tone possible. "Those are just stories people tell each other because they're afraid of death. You have to understand, we know what the universe is made from, and it is atoms, not demons."

"You are going to be fun," he says with a reckless, sexy grin. He's hot. Hotter than any man I've ever dated. He's like a rockstar crossed with a ruthless criminal. It's a pity he's clearly insane.

"Please, be reasonable."

"Reasonable has never really been one of my strong suits," he says. "Sorry about that."

That was my mistake. I am asking someone who believes in angels and demons to be reasonable. He's obviously not capable of that kind of thought. I am being abducted by a madman. What can one do under such circumstances?

I start screaming. I scream and I scream and I do not stop. He's forced to pull the van over to deal with me or risk a ruptured ear drum.

"Okay. Okay. Christ!" He slaps a hand over my mouth and leans in toward me. He still smells really good, and up close his eyes are lit with the kind of sinful dark intensity that makes good girls wake up wondering what happened to them. "You have to settle down. I know this all sounds weird, but it's true, and even if it wasn't true, going off like a fucking fire alarm isn't going to change anything. You get free of me and go to the police, I guarantee you someone shows up within a day with another ceremonial bleeding knife. You are on Fleisch's radar now. Trust me when I tell you that I am the lesser of the evils."

He lets go of my mouth. I start screaming again. Now that I have started, I am not completely sure I know how to stop. I have been terrified for the past three hours and I have barely peeped a word. Now it feels right to scream.

Cosmos slaps his hand across my mouth again.

"You're sort of a slow learner, aren't you. Don't make me spank you."

His words send a bolt of shock and excitement right through me. When he takes his hand away, I seem to have forgotten how to scream.

"Good girl," he praises. I feel another bolt go through me, this one is hotter and cozier. Why do I care about his approval?

"Now," he says. "I'm going to take you back to my hotel room, and you're going to get cleaned up and changed into something that's not pajamas and then we're going to drive to England. It's a ten-hour drive, so don't wear anything fancy."

He really assumes I am just going to go along with all of this.

I do seem to be going along with all of it, though. I sit quietly as he drives me to the hotel. It is a nice hotel. A five-star hotel. A hotel with a rear entrance that allows him to take me up so nobody sees a blood-stained woman. I wonder what other sins this back entrance has hidden over time.

"I will get a doctor to look at that wound," he says. "You may need stitches."

"I don't like doctors. Or needles."

"So you must have really not been fond of that knife, I imagine."

"No," I say.

By this time he has me in his suite. He doesn't look like he belongs in a place like this, with clean carpet and expensive wallpaper. He looks like he should be in some back alley doing a photoshoot for Vogue. Every time I look at him, I feel butterflies erupt in my stomach.

"That wedding, that wasn't real, was it? That's just some kind of ritual to appease your idea of what God is?"

"That's what all weddings are," he says.

"Well, no, some are legally binding and come with obligations."

He shrugs, as if the concept of the law doesn't apply to him. I half believe that it might not. Since he rescued me, I have found myself inhabiting a twilight world of perfect strangeness. I've been wounded, and yet the wound hasn't bothered me since he bandaged it. The adrenaline and the arousal has kept me from being bothered by little things like sliced flesh. I don't know myself when I am in this man's orbit, and that might be the most frightening thing about this entire ordeal. It's not only that he is a stranger to me, it is that he seems to make me a stranger to myself.

"I'm ordering room service. What do you like to eat for breakfast?"

"I don't eat breakfast."

"You do from today."

I don't reply to that. I'm not having breakfast if I don't want to. I do want a shower, though, and to get out of these disgusting blood and now semen-soaked clothes. I grab the clothes I packed in my bag and I go to the shower, locking the door behind me.

I should be at home, in my shower there, getting ready for work. Instead, I'm getting ready for a road trip with my abductor. I turn the shower on and wait for it to get hot, taking my bloody pajamas off. I'm working on a strange sort of auto-pilot. I don't know how to mentally deal with being stabbed, but I do know how to take a shower.

As I wash myself, I feel the ache between my thighs, the sensitivity in my pussy which comes from having given myself to him. It is not that I am in pain, precisely. I am sensitive, and my pussy feels different, somehow, though that is probably just projection because I know that I allowed a man with an impossibly thick, hard cock to ravage me.

"What are you doing, Elise?" I whisper the question to myself as the warm water cascades over me. The shower is the only thing thus far to anchor me to my typical normality. The water is cleansing and the heat is calming and I start to realize I really need to get out of here, go to a doctor and the police, perhaps not in that precise order.

I get out of the shower and dress myself in what I brought with me. It turns out panicked me has a penchant for leggings and tank tops. Both of these are pink. It would be a cute outfit if I was going to the gym. Instead I'm... what am I doing?

I look into the mirror that doesn't steam up because nothing in this place follows the laws of reason. Logically, I know it is because there are coatings that can prevent steam, but in this moment, it just feels like another aberration from normality.

I look pale. Am I always this pale? I washed my hair. I don't know why. I suppose it was the same auto-pilot. My hair hangs almost all the way to my breasts when it is wet. The only bit of color on me is the red seeping through the bandage. The moment I see that flash of red, I start to feel pain. I didn't even notice it before, but now I can feel nothing else. The mind is truly a strange thing.

My cry of pain brings Cosmos through the bathroom door as if the lock wasn't there. He pops it out of the frame itself, causing the kind of damage that hotels take credit card details in advance to cover. He is armed with the same knife he appeared in my apartment with, and his expression is dangerously feral. I let out a shriek and jump backward, forgetting that I must have summoned him with my cry.

He relaxes when he realizes I'm not being attacked. Why does he think I'm going to be in peril several stories up in a bathroom? He is the definition of paranoid or would be if not for the fact that danger seems to surround us. Mostly because we're a danger to ourselves.

"What's wrong?"

"My arm hurts."

"Oh. Yes. Wounds do that. You shouldn't have gotten the bandage wet."

"Would it have made a difference to the pain?"

"No. But it decreases the likelihood of infection."

He speaks of infection and medical care like a perfectly sane human being. It gives me a little glimmer of hope that I might be able to reason with him after all.

Having led me from the bathroom and into the main suite, Cosmos sits me down at the table they probably intended to be used for eating, but inevitably must have been used for all kinds of hotel perversions. He peels the sodden bandage off my arm. It starts bleeding more profusely almost immediately. I turn my head away. I don't like blood. Especially not this kind, the wrong kind coming from the wrong place.

"Don't worry, I'll patch you up."

He's fast and efficient. He has me re-bandaged in what seems like under a minute. I feel better, but the wound still aches.

"Did you go to school for medicine?"

"I was an EMT at one time," he says. "Don't worry, you're in good hands. I'm going to stitch that up."

"You are not."

"I think you'd probably prefer I did, unless you like having a weeping gash on your arm."

"I want to go to a hospital."

"And catch whatever filth is floating about the halls? No. We'll do it here. You'll be fine."

"I don't think I will be, actually."

He cups my face in his hands. "I am never going to let any harm come to you, do you understand? I want you to know that to your very core. You never have to be afraid of anyone or anything again."

"Really? What about climate change?"

He smirks rakishly as I rebuff what would have been a very romantic moment if he wasn't a stranger who just forced me into marriage. I refuse to give into his charms. I know that's what he wants. Men like him are used to taking what they want from women. All he has to do is smile and I bet entire rooms swoon. I know I swooned for him. I spread my legs and I let him take what I was telling myself I was saving for marriage. All it took was a pretend ceremony at some twisted altar and I was ready to fuck him. God. Who am I?

"I know you're a smart woman. I know you work in a laboratory. So I know you're going to try to distract me with thoughts and ideas."

"Heaven forbid," I mutter under my breath. In my experience, men are particularly disdainful of thoughts and ideas when they come from a woman who they'd rather was on her back with her legs open.

"I'm going to put a couple of stitches in and then you can have pancakes."

There's a lilt to his tone that almost makes me feel as though he thinks he's speaking to a child. He is looking for various ways to make me compliant. I've decided I'm going to let him fix my arm, and I've also decided I'm going to have the pancakes. I'm going to need the carbs when I run away from him, which I intend on doing very, very soon. I can't allow him to take me out of the city. Once he does that the chances of escaping are much, much lower.

He has a medical kit ready. I'm a little surprised at how prepared he is given how chaotic he seems to be, but appearances can be deceptive.

"You'll feel a small prick," he says.

"That's unfortunate, given I had no choice in the marriage."

"Don't make me laugh!"

I glance over at him and see him trying not to burst out laughing while holding an uncapped needle of anesthetic. Maybe it's the needle that triggers me, maybe I just sense that opportunity has arisen and I might not get one like it again.

I run. I dash for the door of the suite, and as luck would have it, it's already opening because room service is coming with breakfast. Pancakes fly around me, little saucers of pan-fried batter goodness filling the air as I dash past the elevators and to the stairs.

C osmos

She is a lot faster than I thought she'd be. Nimble too. I'm impressed — but I cannot afford to let her get to the ground floor. The last thing the hotel needs is a bleeding, panicked girl rushing through the lobby. I've paid them to look the other way for a certain amount of shenanigans, but

Elise is a pretty young lady and she will draw the attention of white knights, law enforcement, and Fleisch.

She's skittering down those stairs dangerously fast. I vault the railing and land several feet down, but right in front of her. She lets out a hapless scream as I gather her up in my arms and run back up the stairs with her clutched firmly over my shoulder.

"Let me go! LET ME GO! I'M NOT YOUR WIFE!"

I have an impulse to lay my palm across her ass. She deserves a good spanking for not listening to me, but I know she's just panicking and acting out. My brothers might lay into their women at first provocation, but my authority is not that fragile. I can control her easily. No need to thrash her. Not yet, anyway.

Getting her back into the room is easy, but it's obvious that keeping her is going to be hard. She's just as scared of me as she was of the Fleisch operative, more so now that I've hunted her down physically.

I lock the door, knowing that she has the same access to the lock that I do, and therefore if I take my eye off her for more than thirty seconds, she's going to run again.

She looks at me with tears welling in her eyes. "Why are you doing this to me? I just want to go home."

I thought her sleeping with me was some kind of biological agreement, but obviously she's having second thoughts. The sun being up is not helping. Things that seem sensible in the dead of night are often revealed to be utter madness in the light of day.

"I'm not doing anything to you besides saving your life. Look. There's evidence."

I have a file, found at the Fleisch Laboratory. When I was sent to destroy those who trafficked sacred blood from England, I did a thorough job when it came to eliminating the local threats. I also went through their files and found her details listed in a plain manila folder with vicious intent.

I drop the file on the hotel table in front of her. "There," I say. "Look."

She flips the cover open and glances over the interior. There are several pictures of her taken outside her apartment and her work. There's also an in-depth personal profile. Her age, twenty-five, her country of origin, the USA, her educational history, her family tree, and her current familial status, which is that of a practical orphan. In other words, she is the perfect target for Fleisch.

Her eyes widen. Finally, she might be starting to understand the danger she was in and how orchestrated the whole affair was.

"You have a dossier on me?"

She misses the point with nearly as much alacrity as she ruined the pancakes.

"It's not..." I sigh. "It's not *my* dossier. I found this in the laboratory where you and your blood would have been taken. As soon as I found this file, I knew you'd be the next target. So I came to save you, and just in the nick of time, as it turned out. Now sit down and let me fix your arm up. If you're going to run away, you may as well be some semblance of intact."

She sits and sulks. Maybe she's scared, but there's more to her mood than simple fear. She's annoyed and confused. I suspect with a woman like her, the two moods are closely linked. Some people are afraid of what they don't understand. What Elise doesn't understand angers her.

At least she is sitting still long enough to let me numb her up and run a couple of stitches through the wound. She'll be okay, though there's a decent chance it'll leave a scar. It could have been much worse. There are arteries running not far from this incision point. She's a very lucky young lady.

"You mean there's really an actual laboratory of freaks who believe in angels and demons?"

"Yes. This particular group of freaks believes that your blood can be used to animate the flesh of Christ."

She rolls her eyes. "How could anybody with the funding for a lab be that stupid?"

"Money doesn't imply intelligence. And it may be possible. We don't know. Remember what happened when scientists reanimated dinosaurs?"

"That... that was Jurassic Park. That was a movie. And they didn't reanimate them, they spliced their DNA with gender-bending frogs..."

She is cute when she's almost absolutely exploding with outrage. I can tell I will have a lot of fun teasing my hyper-logical bride.

"You're messing with me," she realizes.

"I am."

"Tell me you're messing with me about the Jesus stuff."

"Oh, I'd never mess with you about the Jesus stuff," I assure her.

She scowls as I put an adhesive bandage over her stitches. "I'd like to sell this group of morons some magical rocks and maybe a harmonic bracelet or some other bullshit."

"You're a skeptic."

"Yes," she says. "I'm a scientist. I'm skeptical of everything that hasn't been proved by the scientific method."

"I see." I can't stop smirking. She's so arrogant, and so certain she knows what the world is made of. She has absolutely no idea, and I know I am going to enjoy watching her deal with all the revelations coming her way. "There," I say. "Almost as good as new."

E*lise*

"You can't keep me against my will."

Sure, he came flying down the stairs like a tattooed puma, in a moment that I'm pretty certain will be forever emblazoned in my mind, a core memory. But he's not always going to be able to chase me down. Not if I'm smart about it — and being smart is my bread and butter.

"Oh, sweet thing, you're so constantly, stridently wrong," he says as if he can hardly stop himself from laughing in my face. "And you're laboring under the intense, persistent delusion you understand the world."

I narrow my eyes at him. He's insulting me now. I know I need to keep my temper, but it would seem that I can take being stabbed. I can take being forced into (fake) marriage. But I cannot abide someone mocking the scientific method. It's a trigger for me.

"I understand the world better than people who run around stabbing women because of angels," I say. "It's nice you saved my life, but I don't consider us married, and I hope you know I'll be escaping and turning you into the police as soon as I can."

His brows are rising as I speak, every threat ratcheting them up a fraction more toward his deep blue hair.

"Wow," he says. "I suppose I better be careful I don't let you escape."

He's toying with me. I can see the glittering amusement in his dark eyes. This man is chaos personified, and I am caught in his influence.

"I ordered more breakfast," he says. "I suggest you eat it instead of turning it into a carpet ornament. I'm going to give you a day or two to come to terms with this, because I know you're a rigid little thing. But your grace period is limited, and I will start to discipline you if you can't do as you are told."

"Oh, discipline me!" I have outrage on my side, making me feel strong. "If you lay so much as a finger on me..."

I am ignoring the fact that he has already laid fingers on me several times, and we both know that.

"Breakfast!" This time the porter announces himself cheer-fully and leaves the cart outside the door.

"Are you going to try to run out the door again? Or are you going to sit there like a good girl and avoid the spanking you deserve?"

That threat makes me tingle — and it makes my blood boil. I don't care if he's hot. I don't care if the idea of being spanked has always been a turn on for me. I absolutely care that this man is taking away my autonomy and replacing it with pancakes.

I watch him as he walks to the door and retrieves the tray of pancakes. He comes back with that same smug smile on his face, the same arrogant set of his chin. I wonder if he's ever been properly and truly told no before. He seems like someone who has always gotten his way with everybody, someone who breaks rules and then pretends they're just not there.

He leans down to put the tray of pancakes down on the table, and something mad takes over me. I don't want to be a subservient, grateful, forced wife. I want to show him he's picked on the wrong girl this time.

As the tray descends toward the table, my hand rises. Force equals mass times acceleration. I slap the thing right out of his hand. Together we watch as a second batch of ill-fated pancakes arc through the air and land on the hotel's carpet. I'm sure they know how to get sticky stuff out of the fibers. For their sake, I truly hope they do.

Cosmos lets out a laugh, and then grabs me by the back of my tank top. Doesn't really offer him much in the way of leverage, but it turns out that doesn't matter, because all he wants to do is sit down in the chair next to me and put me over his thigh.

He slaps my ass. Hard. Hard enough to make me squeal. I feel a flash of heat and a stinging pain that I didn't actually anticipate. I always thought spankings sounded kind of hot. It never occurred to me that they'd really hurt. This one really hurts from the beginning, his hand sweeping through the air time after time and catching my upturned, legging-clad ass in heavy, stern strokes. He doesn't come across like a strict kind of guy, but the evidence now suggests he is.

I am snugged tight against his hard body, unable to squirm away and completely unable to stop him from spanking me. In a desperate attempt to stop the punishment from continuing, I put my hand back to cover my ass. As quickly as I do that, he slaps my open palm and grips my wrist to pull the arm up and away from his target area.

"I don't mind if you want to be a brat," he says. "I love brats. But I also love to make brats very, very sore."

He emphasizes that point with a flurry of slaps right to the seat of my poor posterior. I can't help my reaction. I squirm, and I whimper, and I even find myself begging as the pain gets too intense.

"Please! Okay! I'm sorry!"

He relents instantly, patting instead of smacking, like I am a good pet.

"You think we understand each other? Is it safe to order more pancakes?"

"Yes. Fine. Okay."

He lets me up, putting me back in the chair I started in. My ass lands on the puffy hotel chair and it still hurts even though there's barely any solidity to the chair. It should be like sitting on a cloud. Instead, my rear is aching and throbbing even through the carefully constructed layers protecting it from the cheap laminate that lurks at its core.

"More pancakes."

Cosmos is on the phone. He winks at me as he makes the third order of the day. "Yes. The first two were great. We just love your pancakes. Yes. Newlyweds. Yes. We love pancakes. Oh, yes. Thank you so much."

"Third time lucky?" He gives me a smile as he hangs up the phone.

"Who knows. Maybe."

I am speaking more bravely than I am prepared to act. The heat in my ass has not only chastised me, it has proved to me that he is ready to inflict pain as well as pleasure if he sees fit. He's ruthless.

A tap at the door heralds the news that pancakes are here again. This time, Cosmos is not taking any chances with his breakfast. He tells me to stay seated at the table, goes to the door, opens it, and ushers the porter in.

"Put them on the table," he says. I guess he figures I'm less likely to throw them everywhere in front of a stranger.

The porter puts the pancakes down — and puts a knife to my throat. It all happens so quickly and smoothly I find myself in the kind of shock that doesn't allow me to process these events as real.

"Nice try, brotherhood, but she's ours." The man smirks. I am a fraction of an inch away from death, and in this moment, I find my eyes locking on Cosmos. I don't move. I wait for him to fix this.

Cosmos is not looking at me. His eyes are fixed on the man with the knife, and his expression is terrifying. It is vicious and unfathomably evil. There is anticipation there, a thrill at having an excuse to do something truly terrible.

"Take that knife off her neck now, and I will kill you quickly. If you don't, I will kill you painfully."

The man doesn't take the knife from my neck. He presses it in harder. I feel a trickle of warmth. That's my blood again. Then I feel hot breath and a wet tongue. He's licking my blood from me. It is a grotesque intimacy that makes me shudder.

Cosmos turns his gaze to me. "Ready to admit you might be targeted by a blood-obsessed cult of messianic scientists?"

I nod as much as I dare, which is not much at all, but he picks up the gesture, and the room explodes.

He moves much faster than anybody should be able to, turning to a blur of man and tattoo. The knife clatters onto the table. The man who was holding it hits the wall, cracking the plaster.

Then things get messy. I look, and then wish I hadn't, and then I look again, and then I look away. What Cosmos is doing is wrong and nasty, and entirely what he promised to do. He looks up, catches me looking, and shakes his head curtly.

"Go into the bathroom," he says, "and put the complimentary earplugs in."

"Cosmos..."

"Do it. Now."

I do as I am told.

Earplugs don't cut out enough sound. So I run the shower, and I turn on the complimentary radio, and I try to pretend that the discordant shrieking coming through the bathroom is just some new kind of music. In a way, it is.

I'm still trying to come to terms with the events of the day, but no sooner do I process one thing than something else even more terrible happens. I am in the company of a man who knows how to torture and kill, and who has done both in my presence. I am the target of people with some mad delusion. I have been ripped out of consensus reality, and I do not know what to do with myself.

I have another shower. I need to clean myself in a way I have never been cleaned before. The filth of these deeds is clinging to me on the inside, as if it penetrated my skin and got into some ephemeral part of my being.

Some time later, Cosmos opens the door to the bathroom. I am naked in the shower. Mist might hide me but probably doesn't. He's seeing me naked for the first time, but he doesn't stop for long to take the sight in. He is too busy stripping off his own blood-soaked clothing. I see him come into view through the haze. Tattoos truly do cover most all of his arms and his powerful thighs. They range across his chest and just barely take a break down the muscular plane of his abdomen. His cock is thick and heavy, hanging semi-erect from a pelt of sleek black hair. Every part of him is incredible, but it is that cock I can't keep my eyes off.

He washes his hands in the sink, and I am treated to the rear view. His ass is devoid of tattoos, though most of his back is a canvas of what looks to me like mythological stories. When his hands have been cleansed of the sanguine essence of the attacker, he turns to me. "Mind if I get in?"

"I'll, uhm... can you pass me a towel?"

He pretends to preserve my modesty, as if he hasn't seen absolutely everything already, holding a towel out for me and enveloping me in it before taking the shower himself. I stay and watch him as he showers. Partly because his tattooed musculature looks very good under water, but mostly because I don't want to go out into the hotel room and see what he has done. I know it was bad.

My bag is still in here from the first shower I took, but I'm even further down on clothing now. I don't know what I was thinking when I packed. Maybe that I was going to go to work? I find some underwear and a lab coat. I don't have anything else.

"Well," I say. "Fuck."

3

We leave the hotel room full of blood, viscera, and pancake syrup.

"That's a real fucking downer," Cosmos sighs as he bundles me into an expensive-looking black sedan. I wonder what happened to the van.

"Which part, the trail of bodies, or the fact you never got to eat your pancakes?"

"Pancakes, of course." He smiles at me and I feel like laughing. I shouldn't be laughing. I think I've seen two men die today. I've been stabbed. I've had someone else's blood cover me. I've ruined two sets of clothes. I think I might be going slightly mad.

"They're going to call the police," I say as we drive out of Heidelberg on the first leg of our journey.

"I'm having the room cleaned. Don't worry about it. Those rooms are all externally soundproofed, and my team will leave the place pristine."

"It's that easy for you to kill someone?"

"He came for you, Elise," Cosmos says. "I'll kill anybody who lays a hand on you. Fleisch need to understand that you are not an easy target. You're mine, for eternity."

He's so absolutely serious. I wonder how a man like him can make such a complete and total commitment within hours of meeting me. It's not because he loves me. He can't. He doesn't even know me. He is dedicated to me for the same reason those other maniacs are trying to kill me. It's all about this angel blood.

I find myself a little jealous of this nebulous nonsense. If Cosmos wasn't clearly a homicidal maniac with extremist radical tendencies, he'd be my type. Hot is my type. Sexy is my type. And I think crazy might be my type too.

"So," I say, humoring him, which seems like a bright thing to do. "Tell me about this angel blood — and why anyone would think I have it."

"Short version..." He flexes his hands on the steering wheel. They're both bandaged across the knuckles, because of all the punching he was doing. "Angels used to mate with people regularly. Angel blood lies in several human bloodlines to this day. People with it find themselves with powers, sometimes."

I ignore the part about powers because that's clearly mad.

"So you're referring to something genetic."

"No. It's not in the DNA."

"But DNA is the only way we pass information from one generation to the next."

"It's not the only way. There are plenty of demons passed through familial lines. Why not angelic influence as well?"

I don't know if I agree with that premise. I sit, silent and disapproving.

He sighs. "You've seen the men trying to kill you."

"Yes. I believe there are madmen ready to kill for the slightest reason. That doesn't make this angel blood thing any more real."

Cosmos shrugs and falls silent. He can't produce evidence because there isn't any evidence. There's just wild speculation and bald belief. I sit back, feeling slightly more in control than I did before. There's something just so very satisfying about telling someone how very wrong they are about something or other.

"We need breakfast," he says. "I'm going to pull into one of the rest stops off the autobahn once we get on it."

He's a little more serious and subdued now. I wonder if it is the sting of my logic or the repeated killings of the day. It's so strange, I always thought I'd be more hysterical if I saw something like that. But when it's really happening it just sort of doesn't feel real. A human body turns into a general mixture of slushy parts surprisingly quickly under the blade of a skilled killer.

A yawn creeps up on me. I'm tired. I was woken up very early. All this madness unfolded before nine in the morning, and frankly, I don't think I can keep up with it. As we drive into the well risen sun, I close my eyes and take a little nap.

· · ·

C*osmos*

She's cute when she's asleep. It's only when she's speaking that she's an obnoxious little brat who deserves to be spanked long and hard. Turning her over my knee in the hotel room was very satisfying.

She's probably afraid of me. She saw what I did to the second attacker, the harsh and terrible lesson I taught him for the sin of touching her and defying me. Our marriage might not mean much to Elise yet, but it means everything to me.

Fleisch did their research well enough that I feel as though I know her. I know that she is alone in the world. She was raised by a single mother, who is now hospitalized in Maryland. Elise has been living and working in Germany for the past three years. Half her wages go toward paying for her mother's care home, and the other half to her meager living expenses. Her apartment was not well appointed, and she doesn't own much in the way of fancy clothing or possessions. She's been looking after her mother since she was a teenager.

She does not know who her father is, but Fleisch did. I know because she was fathered by one of the more prolific angels who kept a record of all women he mated. Her mother's name was on his list, a document unearthed by Fleisch and used to find the hapless descendants of what now seem to be careless unions.

Elise's entire worldview is based on the notion that there's nothing other than the basic mundane. That is all she has ever experienced. The basic, and the mundane. She's never touched the transcendental. And she's never experienced anybody caring for her. That means there are two challenges I have to overcome with my bride. Yes, I have technically only known her for a matter of hours, but unlike Elise, I do have faith. That faith is part of a series of sensitivities that make me an excellent fighter and an even better lover. I knew the moment I laid eyes on her that she was mine. It was a certainty I felt at the very core of me. She can't feel that knowing. She will have to fall in love slowly and probably painfully. The sadist in me will enjoy that, and the masochist in her will flower awake.

My stomach growls as a gas station sign looms, letting me know that the next turn off represents food. Hunger is one of my least favorite kinds of suffering. It is so unnecessary, and it weakens the body. I chuckle to myself as I remember the wasting of the previous three attempts at breakfast. To lose one set of pancakes was misfortune, but three batches? That was carelessness.

I look over at Elise as I pull into the parking lot. She's still fast asleep. It would be a pity to wake her, but it would probably be madness to leave her completely unattended. It won't take long to order breakfast, and I do want her to sleep... I tap my finger against the steering wheel. Decisions, decisions.

Elise

I wake up in a strange car, in a parking lot I don't recognize.

The events of the morning come flooding back to me, feeling stranger than ever. Did any of that happen? Am I having some kind of breakdown? The latter option feels like it's more of a possibility. It's more likely I went mad and ended up stealing a car and passing out in a parking lot than

I was attacked in my apartment and then again in a hotel room, and…

"What the fuck!"

I try to get out of the car only to discover that I have been chained to the steering wheel. The keys have been taken, and there's a note down in the little center console from the man of what I thought must have been my dreams. It's written in a bold and scrawling hand. "BE BACK SOON, DARLING."

Darling. I've never had anybody call me darling before. The word hits different when you're chained to a car, though. Not exactly as romantic as it might otherwise have been.

Suddenly, he's back.

"Sorry, took longer than I thought. Pancakes are not that hard to make," he says, swinging a long leg into the car. He's wearing ripped jeans, but I don't think they're the pre-distressed kind. This is a man who rips jeans like he rips people. He's a syrup smelling, ultra-hot, super dangerous, absolute maniac and now he is sitting less than a foot from me, offering me pancakes in a cardboard box plate, replete with syrup. There's a wooden fork with it, flimsy but more than up to the task of handling pancakes.

"Are you going to uncuff me?"

Cosmos glances over at the cuffs as if he's noticing that they're a problem for the first time.

"Oh. Yes. Sure. Unless you like them?" He finishes the question with a rakish wink.

I am not amused.

"No, Cosmos — and that's obviously not your real name. I don't like being chained to a steering wheel while I'm asleep. What if something happened? What if a car hit this car and I couldn't get out and I fucking burned alive because you're a possessive maniac?"

He gives me a long, serious look. I'm waiting for him to tell me he's going to spank me again for disrespect or something like that.

"You're right," he says, reaching for his keys. "I'm sorry. I should have been more careful. I don't ever want to be the one who puts you in danger."

It's almost sweet, the way he uncuffs me quickly, a look of real shame on his handsome face.

"Here," he says, handing me my little pancake tray. "I know you don't like breakfast, but it's closer to lunchtime now, so you should be good to eat."

"Thank you," I say, rubbing my wrist where the steel sat against my skin.

We eat. Or, he eats. I pick. I'm trying to come to terms with everything that just assaulted me in my memories. There was so much blood. My blood. Other people's blood.

"I don't think I can eat this," I apologize.

"What's wrong?"

"I just feel a little queasy."

His concern is genuine, even if it comes from a crazy place.

"What else do you want? A salad? A sandwich? Crackers? Juice? Rice?"

"I'm okay. I don't usually eat until dinner time."

He frowns. "That's not healthy."

"You just wolfed down six gas station pancakes, don't talk to me about healthy."

"True," he admits. "But you are going to eat something at our next stop."

"Deal," I say.

He starts the car and we are off again on the open road. The autobahn is a thing of beauty, wide open stretches of road that seem to go on forever. I rest my head against the back of the seat and surrender to the madness, just for a little bit. This is going to be a long drive to...

"Where are we going?"

"A safe place. It's like an ancestral home for people like me. You will be safe there, with the other wives."

"Oh, so there are other kidnapped women?"

"No. You're the only one who has technically been kidnapped, far as I'm aware. I heard Thor has found some female to entertain his hammer."

"Thor. The Norse god?"

"He's not a god. He's just a big blond Norwegian-ish guy."

"Who else is there?"

"Well, there's Bryn. Unfortunately."

"You don't like Bryn?"

"His family owns the manor, and he thinks he's our leader. He's not. He breaks rules."

Cosmos sounds deeply offended by that, and that surprises me.

"You don't seem like the sort of person to be upset by rule breaking."

"Some rules can be broken. Others mean something. He's a demon-summoning bastard."

"Why are we going to stay somewhere where the man who owns it is someone you hate? Sounds like he's your anti-pancake."

"Anti-pancake," he laughs. "Yeah. He's an anti-pancake, alright."

We drive a few more miles before he elaborates again.

"It's called Direview Manor," he says. "And it's a nice place. Or it could be. You'll find it interesting."

"I need my job," I tell him. "I have responsibilities. They're not going to fire me for missing today, but they will fire me if I run off to an English Manor without notice. My mom depends on me to pay for her care. I can't afford to be unemployed."

"I know. I'm going to make sure she's taken care of. I have money, unlike the poor boys at Direview. You don't have to work anymore. And you don't have to worry about providing for your mother. I'm going to look after my family."

His family. We met six hours ago, at most. And he's prepared to pay for my mother's home and let me retire into a life of alleged luxury.

"Why... why are you doing this? I mean, I think you're crazy, but you can't be this functional *and* crazy unless you have a very specific illness, and I'm not picking up on any indicators of specific..."

"You're my wife," he says.

"Right, but you married me within twenty minutes of knowing me. There's no way you could have fallen in love that quick. It's not possible."

"Yes. It is. I loved you the moment I saw you."

He says it with such conviction I almost believe him, except I can't believe him. Because that's not how real feelings work. I'm just an idea to him. I'm a bag of special blood. Maybe he thinks he loves me, but that's not possible. Nobody loves me that way. I'm not the sort of girl men fall in love with. I'm the sort of girl they ignore. I'm mousy, and pale, and yes, I am blonde, but that alone doesn't get you far when you're an unglamorous, angular, stiff, and sometimes even unpleasantly logical woman who points out the flaws in jokes rather than laughs at them.

I know I need to get away from him. Whatever is waiting for me in England it's not solid enough to bet my mother's life on. She needs round-the-clock care, and the facility is not understanding about missed bills.

He knows about that too. Must have been in the dossier. Those creeps had a very detailed dossier. Seems like a waste to compile all that information just to stab someone, but what do I know.

"You might be the sort to fall in love right away and marry someone and take care of their mom, but I'm not that... impulsive." I'm proud of myself for finding the right word.

"I know," he says. "I don't expect anything from you besides your obedience."

"What?"

"Your love won't come easy. Everything will take time. The only thing I can't compromise on or give you more time for, is doing as you're told when it comes to your safety."

He almost sounds reasonable. Except, of course, he also sounds overbearing and intense. Because that's who he is.

"When we get to Direview, you're going to start learning how to defend yourself. You're not going to be able to stop an attacker, necessarily, but you can at least avoid being stabbed for slightly longer than the last two times. You're a sitting duck for Fleisch. You need to learn to move."

"I was asleep when the first man came."

"And you're not going to be caught sleeping again, because I'll be with you."

There's some comfort in that. Having a big, strong, maniac of a man beside me always, looking after me. Keeping me from being hurt. Loving me, even if it's for weird and delusional reasons. My logical side, the strongest side of me, makes me think that this is not the absolute worst of circumstances a girl could find herself in. Maybe... maybe it wouldn't hurt to give him a chance.

Then I remember the blood, and what he was doing to the man who tried to stab me. Cosmos is not a harmless eccentric. He's a harmful eccentric. A really dangerous one. And that's where the logical part of me steps in again, telling me in no uncertain terms that I cannot let him take me to this Direview Manor. I just have to wait for a good opportunity to escape.

I'll let him take me to England. My passport is in my bag, and I always have enough money in my savings account for a ticket to the States. I'll fly back the USA, make sure mom is okay, and hope that my job will take me back. I really need to call them and make my excuses. They'll understand a family emergency. I can see Mom, make sure she's okay, and then go back to work, or maybe apply for a transfer. My company is multinational with branches across the globe. I could take a position somewhere nobody knows me, and nobody can find me.

I'm starting to feel better. I have something like a plan, and a plan is power. Maybe not the kind of power you get from being able to avoid stabbings and inflict damage yourself, but a different kind of power. Possibly a more powerful one.

Ten hours of driving is not actually as long as you think it is. After a while, the hours start to blur and countries turn into other countries. Germany turns to Belgium, becomes France briefly, and then we're under a massive body of water, being carried like a torpedo toward what he would call destiny and I would call England.

Dover is where I make the call. I've been steeling my nerves this whole time. The forty minutes in the train for cars during which Cosmos took a nap, knowing there was nowhere for me to go, I worked myself up to it.

"Are we going to stop for food? I'm hungry."

"Finally getting an appetite? It's that English port air," Cosmos says.

We're both foreigners in this country. Neither one of us belongs here. I wonder if Cosmos really belongs anywhere. He's a very strange man and an interesting one. There is a part of me that would like to get to know him more. But there's a bigger part that just wants to be free of all this oddness and find normality again. I miss my mom.

"They have some decent fish and chips," he says. "Greasy food, but it's something. Wait in the car. I'll get us some and we can drive to overlook the Channel. It'll be romantic."

Romantic isn't exactly how I would describe this road trip. It is more like an abduction with extra steps. But I force something like a smile to my lips. It's better if he thinks I am coming around.

He winks and leaves me in the parked car.

There's not that many people around. It's around seven in the evening, and he's parked us in a quiet alley. I know I only have a few minutes at most to make my escape, so the second I'm sure Cosmos is gone, I grab my bag and I sneak away.

Unfortunately, I have no idea where I am, and the English are fond of old maze-like streets and alleys that go in all directions at once. It would be charming if I was on holiday, but as I am trying to run away, it just makes everything that much more difficult.

I see a bland-looking stranger on a corner, a man wearing a beige overcoat and a matching cap. He could be the hero in a hard-boiled detective novel, but I'm willing to bet he's not.

"Excuse me, do you know where the airport is?"

The man raises a brow at me upon hearing my American accent. "You're in the wrong town for a plane," he says. "You'd need to take the train to Southend."

"Oh. Well. Where's the train station, then?"

"From here…"

"Darling!" A heavy hand comes down on my shoulder. Cosmos has found me. He has a white newsprint-wrapped package under his arm, and he looks very composed given how mad I know he must be. How the hell was he that fast?

"Don't mind her, she's always lost!" Cosmos says. "I found us some dinner, darling."

There's a moment in which I could beg the dour stranger for help, and then the moment passes. His eyes drop, his interest wanes, and I become just another oddly clad tourist. He didn't even seem to notice that I am wearing a lab coat.

"I warned you," Cosmos growls in my ear as he escorts me back to the car. "Running away is very naughty, Elise. I won't have it."

Is it just me, or does he sound more English just for being here? Sussing out Cosmos' true nature, nationality, or intentions is nearly impossible. He marches me back to the car as cheerfully as possible. We make a very odd pair, him with his tattoos and his rough attire, and me in my lab coat. Surely someone around us notices? Surely someone will step in?

Nobody does. They have their eyes to the pavement or their phones, and they barely see me as Cosmos takes me up that fateful alley.

"How did they cook food that fast?"

"They don't cook it to order. They cook it and it sits under heat lamps."

"Well, that's fucking disgusting," I say.

"I agree," he says. "Indicates a fundamental lack of understanding of what food should be, either hot, fresh, or both. But I digress." He pops the trunk. "Get in."

"What?" I stare at him, shocked.

"You can't be trusted to ride like a normal person, so you can ride in the trunk"

"I'm not getting in…"

Next thing I know he's just sort of tossing me in there. The trunk is more spacious than I expected it to be. It's also cleaner, which is nice. He pulls out a black canvas bag as he puts me in. I wonder what's in it. Seems sort of heavy, like a bowling ball. Does he like bowling? And is he really going to force me to travel in the trunk?

"Remember how you said you'd never put me in danger? This is very dangerous. If you get rear-ended, I am going to be paste in this all-weather fabric lining."

"I'll be careful about other cars and their following distances," he says, cold as ice. From inside the trunk, looking up at him looking down at me, there's a certain mercilessness about his features and expression that sends a terrifying but borderline erotic sensation spearing through to the very core of me.

"Don't close the trunk," I beg him. "Don't…"

CLANG!

It is louder than I thought it would be. For a good minute or two I am shrouded in a complete darkness that makes me want to scream. I don't like the dark. I've never trusted it, and I trust it even less now.

I hear him get into the driver's seat. He is not going to drive me like this, is he? It's so unsafe. There's no seatbelt, there's not even a seat, and if we get hit, this is all crumple zone.

There's a flash of light as he reaches into the back and pulls down the little arm rest that nobody ever uses between the back seats. That lets me see into the vehicle, and he adjusts his rear-view mirror so he can't see the road behind him at all anymore. He can only see me.

"You're a bad girl," he says conversationally as we set off yet again. "Don't worry. It's not far to Direview now. I'll deal with you then."

"You're a maniac," I tell him. "And I'm never going to be your wife. Not ever."

I have been compliant long enough. I have tried to placate him long enough. Fuck that. This ends now. No more kidnapping. No more fucking Ms Nice Captive.

I start to kick at the tail light. I heard once that you can do that if you're ever abducted and put in a trunk, and then you can stick a hand or a foot out and alert people to the extreme fuckery that's going on.

The only problem with that plan is the fact that my kidnapper has that little portal down, and he hears what I'm doing right away. I expect him to tell me to cut it out, but he swings the car over and pulls to a halt.

"You're trying my patience," he tells me as he opens the trunk. As he does, I discover that we're in a picturesque layby. There are willow trees overhead. That means there's probably water too, a river or something. Funny how these useless and irrelevant factoids keep popping into my head even as my captor pulls out lengths of hemp rope, from what I have to assume is an abduction kit, to tie me hand and foot.

He works quickly and deftly. He's done this before. He knows just how tight to make the rope so it stays on and constricts but doesn't actually hurt me.

"If you fight those knots, they'll tighten," he says.

"Safety first," I remind him with enough snark to sink a ship.

And then he gags me. As he wraps him-smelling fabric around the back of my neck through my mouth, I consider that I might have made a mistake. It's too late now, though. The trunk closes, and my fate is sealed.

4

C*richton*

There is a certain kind of calm at Direview that only ever settles over the place when all the men in residence are happily coupled. We are enjoying that period of time now. It is a pleasant sort of easiness, in which domestic affairs take precedence. For the moment, the roof still leaks, but a bucket or thirty have been deputized to deal with those issues.

A meeting of the Brotherhood has become more of a family gathering over a hearty meal. I used to do all the cooking, but Crocombe puts so much stock into her offerings, poor dear, I let her do all the kitchen labor now.

It is a sunny Sunday afternoon, around about three o'clock, which as every civilized person knows, is time for a little something. Bryn and Nina, Thor and Anita are all taking tea in the conservatory that opens up onto the garden. I have spent some time among the roses and am pleased with both the scent and sight of them, not to mention the bespoke rosewater I make from them.

"HELLO! ANYBODY HOME!?"

The cry comes from the front door and is accompanied by heavy footsteps and a general bashing about the place that can only herald one person.

We look up as Cosmos walks in with a hemp bag containing something heavy, and apparently, bloody. He dumps it on the long table and looks around at us all with a broad grin. This man is a stone-cold maniac. There is no other way to describe him. From his blue hair to his many tattoos, to the reckless tendency to violence and murder, he is a liability — except if you happen to be an organization of demon hunters. Then he's an asset, albeit one likely to go rogue at any time.

"And what's this, then?"

"This is the head of Fleisch."

Cosmos is ever so pleased with that little play on words. I allow myself a gentle smile of acknowledgement while Nina blanches and attempts to distance herself from the gory sight. I am almost entirely certain that Anita is going to try to poke the bag with something, most likely her finger judging by the way it creeps across the table. Thor slaps her hand away at the last minute, earning himself both a glare and a pout.

"We're always trying to stop them from using angelic blood to animate whatever side of beef they think is the body of Christ. So I went there, and I killed the man in charge. Problem solved."

"Except for the fact there will inevitably be someone waiting in the wings to take over."

Cosmos narrows his eyes at Bryn. The two have never gotten along. I have to admit I am curious as to why Cosmos has decided to return after declaring he would absolutely do no such thing under any circumstances whatsoever.

"I'll cut his head off too. I've got an endless supply of blades fit for the purpose. It's heads all the way down. And I found something else. It's in the back of the car."

We follow with no small amount of trepidation, all the gang traipsing out to the vehicle which stands with the driver's door still open and a small pool of blood on the passenger seat where the head must have once sat.

He opens the boot of the car and reveals a young woman, perhaps twenty years or so of age. She has pale blonde hair and ice blue eyes and a diminutive frame that speaks to having had very little to eat in quite some time. Her wan, terrified expression and wide eyes elicit the greatest of pity.

"Who is this?" Bryn asks the question.

"Oh," Cosmos grins broadly. "This is my wife."

"Why is your wife tied up in the fucking trunk, you psychopath?" Nina has erupted in outrage, her face instantly nearly as red as her hair.

Cosmos seems momentarily confused. "I... I don't know. This is just how I usually travel with people."

"You're a fucking nutter," Anita exclaims. "A proper fucking bellend."

Together, the girls help Cosmos' captive out of the car. Anita has a knife on her that she uses to cut the bindings. I see Thor's brow rise as she produces the blade. He should know a demoness will always be prepared to do what is necessary.

The poor thing is shaking like a leaf. It is not common, or in any way acceptable, for the Brotherhood to endorse violence against the gentler sex. Though both Nina and Anita are high spirited at times and receive the appropriate corrections, neither of them has ever been treated in this callous a manner.

"You've gone too far this time, mate," Bryn announces, wrapping him up in a headlock and dragging him away. Cosmos takes this feedback by attempting to punch Bryn in the kidneys as hard as he can, while cursing at the top of his lungs. I find myself yearning for the old days, where clearer heads and maturer mindsets prevailed. But the old Brotherhood was perverted and corrupt. At least this young blood is passionate in their cause.

Mrs Crocombe comes bustling out of the house with some hot tea, scones, jam, and cream. She has an unerring instinct for knowing when someone in the area needs a cream tea.

"There you are," she says, greeting the girl as if she has known her her whole life. "Why don't you come in and have some tea?"

"Ich möchte nach Hause gehen," the girl whimpers.

"She's German," Anita announces, as if that is a piece of information not immediately obvious to everybody.

"Do you speak English?" Nina asks kindly.

"I'm not German. It's just habit," the young lady replies. She is fiddling with her long blonde hair nervously, avoiding the gazes of all present. Hardly surprising, given her obvious trauma. An unplanned interlude with Cosmos would test the nerves of even the most hardened of maidens, and it is clear she does not fall into that category.

"What's your name?"

"Elise."

"Pretty name," Nina says. "Come with us, Elise. We will make sure he doesn't hurt you anymore. Bryn's thrashing him right now, I bet."

"He's a very bad man," Elise whimpers. "He's a very, very bad man."

"Extra cream," Mrs Crocombe declares. "That's what you need. Feeding up."

If only cheerfulness, a stiff upper lip, and lashings of cream were enough to fix the mess Cosmos has made with his careless, brutal behavior. I have the sense there is a tangled web here that will be more difficult to unravel than anybody suspects.

Cosmos

"Let me go, you moron," I curse at Bryn. "I've brought you the head of Fleisch and saved one of the angel lines. You could try a 'thank you, Cosmos, good job, Cosmos.'"

"You married a woman against her will?"

"I had to."

"Why?"

"Because she didn't want me to marry her with her will, and obviously we had to marry so I could protect her bloodline, so..."

Bryn's glaring at me. I hate this man at the best of times. He's so overbearing, and believes himself beyond reproach, when in reality he is one of the worst of us. I knew he'd get his knickers in a knot as soon as he saw the head, and of course he has to pretend he cares about Elise without even knowing her.

"Do you try to be as unhinged as humanly possible, is that it? Or does it come naturally?"

He has a certain biting Englishness that has always gotten under my skin. I could take a punch in the face and laugh it off, but these snide comments are almost more than I can take without punching him in the face.

"I killed their leader, I destroyed their offices, I found their target, and I saved her. You might not like how I did it, but I did it. While you were holed up here with your wife, I claimed mine."

Bryn draws in a breath, then sighs. "You're right."

"I am?" I try not to sound surprised.

"A hundred percent. I asked you to do something, and you did it. Just tell me you didn't... hurt the girl."

He doesn't mean hurt. He means something so much worse.

"No. Bryn. I'm not a rapist. Thanks for checking."

"Alright," he says. "Then we don't have a problem."

. . .

E *lise*

I have been embraced by two young women similar in age to me. It's a warmer welcome than I expected.

"Cosmos is intense," the redhead says.

"I've known him for all of five minutes and I can say he's crazier than a demon," the dark haired one says. I know that I should know their names. I think one is called Anita, the darker, shorter one. And the other one, the beautiful willowy supermodel type.... oh, that's right. Nina.

They've hustled me off to an old stone kitchen. This place is astonishing. I have been in a lot of older buildings, but this place is charged with history in a way like no other place I've ever been in.

Mrs Crocombe is waiting for us with a fresh batch of afternoon tea. She looks like she stepped out of a fairytale. She has an apron and an old-fashioned hat that helps pin down her graying hair. There's warmth to her, but that warmth is not without edge.

She presents a spread of food I can only describe as a small banquet and bids me eat.

"Thank you," I say, being polite out of force of habit. "It all smells wonderful."

"I'll get you a plate," she says. "Don't worry, you'll feel much better after you've had something to eat."

I don't know if that is true, but I am starving. Whether I'll feel better or not, I have to eat.

"Tell us what happened," Nina says. "I know it will seem strange."

"He believes in angels and demons," I blurt. "He's crazy. I don't mean he believes in them as a harmless religious abstract that could be tolerated by the general public without much in the way of concern. I mean he straight up seriously believes that I have the blood of an angel in me. He needs to be committed."

There's a silence following my outburst, a silence in which I feel a deep awkwardness come over the room. Oh my... what if they all believe in the same thing? He did basically tell me he was taking me into the heart of a cult.

"I know, it's fucking weird." Anita has an attitude, and a local accent. Nina seems to be like me and Cosmos, American, or at least, American enough to have an accent that sets us apart from Europeans.

"But?"

I can hear that word.

"Well, it's true," she says, bluntly.

"I thought it was strange when I first heard it too," Nina says. "The idea that I could have angelic blood in my veins, my real father cuckolded by an angel..."

Folie a deux, or in this case, Folie a everybody. They're all suffering under the same shared delusion. I know I'm not going to be able to argue them out of it. You can't logic people out of a place that logic didn't get them into.

"It is strange," I say.

"Get some food into you, and you'll feel better," Mrs Crocombe says, presenting a big platter of scones, jam, and cream.

They want me to swallow their angel bullshit along with whatever they serve. I can't trust anyone here, no matter how friendly they might seem to be. But I do have to keep up the appearance of being somewhat convinced. I don't want them to be suspicious of me, or to suspect just how delusional I believe they are.

As far as I am concerned, I have just been kidnapped by a cult. Like my generic expectations of cults, they're overly friendly and apparently very concerned with my wellbeing. It's best to play along for now.

"Ah, there you are."

Cosmos appears, apparently unharmed by his arch cult-rival. He smiles at me, but I don't smile back.

"I don't believe we've met," Anita says sticking her hand out to Cosmos. "I'm Anita. I'm Thor's whatever."

"Hello, Thor's whatever," Cosmos says. "Nice to meet you."

Just as Cosmos takes Anita's hand to shake it, a massive blond man comes racing into the kitchen, sweeping Anita up off her feet and away from Cosmos. He looks worried, as if he's afraid Cosmos will hurt her. That's concerning. If the men here don't trust him, then he might be dangerous to me after all.

"What's..."

Cosmos looks at his hand, then at the monstrously-sized blond man. "So we're just a demon nest now."

"Bryn has come to accept her, and you told us you were never returning. If you harm so much as a hair on Anita's head, I will crush you. And then I will summon you back from the hell you so desperately deserve, and I will torture you for the entire span of my life."

The threats are made viciously, in a deep voice tinged with an unmistakable Norwegian lilt. They're serious too, though they sound outlandish. These people truly believe in their collective madness.

"'Ere! That's no way to talk among the ladies!" Mrs Crocombe has fisted a rolling pin, and her jocund expression has turned to one of intense ire. "If you boys have a problem, you know to take it downstairs."

"Yes," Cosmos says. "Let's take it downstairs."

Now everybody seems angry and I'm not entirely sure why, except deduction tells me that offense has been taken because Anita has been designated demonic in their worldview.

Nina and Anita watch as the blond man and Cosmos head to the back of the kitchen and then down the stairs.

"What's down there?"

"Oh, it's like an arena. Full of weapons," Nina says.

"And a prison," Anita adds. "With cells."

"This place has a dungeon?"

"Dungeon. That's a better word," Anita says cheerfully. "Anyway, that's where they're going. To the dungeon. To fight."

"Over you?"

"I'm not the angelic type," Anita says, as if that explains something. She looks like the unemployed type, if I am to be judgmental. She's wearing black jeans and a dark blue hooded sweater. Her dark hair is tied up behind her head. She has the air of someone who doesn't work for their money so much as scam for it. I am making a lot of snap judgements about her, but when you have no context, snap judgements are all you have. Nina is delicate and refined, very pretty. It makes sense she would be married to the head of this mess. She hasn't said that she is, but I would put money on it. She has that ephemeral quality that probably makes her irresistible to men. This is a cult with some very good-looking people in it. Maybe I should be flattered I was picked to join.

"So you have to have angel blood to live here?"

"No, but it helps," Anita snaps sassily.

"There are all sorts here," Nina says in a way that is supposed to be comforting, I think.

There are dull thuds coming from downstairs. They're very muffled, suggesting that if one were down there, one would find them very loud. Given what I have seen Cosmos to do his enemies, I worry for Thor's safety.

"I hope being Thor's whatever doesn't mean you're overly attached to him," I say. "Because from what I've seen, nobody has a chance against Cosmos."

"I think Thor can take care of himself," Anita smirks knowingly.

"Well, from what I have seen, nobody has a chance of survival once Cosmos attacks."

"You've probably seen very little," Anita replies. She seems a tad defensive. Do I seem a tad defensive? Are we doing the adult female version of the schoolyard *my dad could beat up your dad* argument? It would seem so. I'm not going to continue it on, I can already tell that I am making something akin to an enemy here in the cult.

"Where are Cosmos and Thor?" A masculine voice interrupts our conversation. It comes from a man with a heavy presence. I can actually feel the energy in the air change as he walks into the kitchen, and scientifically that's not possible, so that's how much of a complete downer he is.

"Oh. Bryn! This is Elise!" Anita introduces me to the man with the shaggy dark hair and the deep, hollow eyes.

"Yes. Cosmos' wife. Congratulations, and welcome."

"At three o'clock this morning I was woken by someone trying to stab me, and then I was dragged to an altar to be married. I don't know if it is congratulations that are in order. Maybe a mental health assessment for your friend, and some help for me to return home."

Bryn listens with a concerned expression on his face. "You do not want to be married."

"No. I don't. And I don't want to be here. Thank you very much for the hospitality, but I have a life and people who depend on me, and I can't disappear into a den of fucking cultists."

I've lost my temper. That's unfortunate. But it has been a very long day, and I am very hungry, and frankly, I'm at the end of my tether. Those present look at one another and there is the sort of long and poignant silence that doesn't bode well, until a burst of amusement breaks the tension.

Anita laughs. "Fucking cultists. She's not wrong."

"Yes, thank you, Anita," Bryn growls. "I'm sorry your arrival here wasn't easier on you," he says to me. "Cosmos is not the easiest man to get along with and I can well imagine the kind of trauma you may have suffered in coming here. But I can't let you go."

"You can't keep me against my will, either."

"Well...." He tilts his head and gives me a slight shoulder shrug. "That's slightly more debatable, but not the ideal outcome. We will deal with any practical matters that need to be handled. You'll be fine."

"Oh, I'll be fine? Oh, well, that's alright then, isn't it. I didn't know that I would be fine. If only I'd known all along that I was just going to be fine!"

My sarcasm is not lost on those present. Bryn looks displeased. I see Nina reach out and put a calming hand on his arm and watch as he takes a self-soothing breath. I'm impressed at the influence she has over him. He must love her a lot.

"I know you're unhappy," he says. "But Anita and Nina will help you."

"Thank you, but I don't need any handmaidens to show me how to integrate into the cult. I'd just like to know where the front door is."

Bryn's jaw tightens again. He probably wants to hit me. That's how Cosmos deals with a sassy woman, after all. It's probably customary in their cult to beat their women into submission — though to be fair, neither Nina nor Anita come across as beaten-down women.

"Crocombe, is there any popcorn?" Anita chimes in with a loud hissing whisper that does nothing to defuse the situation. Mrs Crocombe aims a swat at Anita, along with a promise to box her ears, which I can only hope means smack and not actually encase in cardboard. Anita dodges the swat with a big grin. She's quite likable, actually.

"Where is Cosmos?" Bryn asks the question impatiently. He's reached the limit of his patience with me, I think.

"Cosmos and Thor are beating each other up downstairs."

"Because that's a sensible thing to do when we have a new arrival," Bryn sighs.

"Cosmos would quite like to kill me," Anita says cheerfully.

"A sentiment shared by many, no doubt," Bryn replies, though he does so with a wink.

There is real warmth here among these people. Pity they're all wildly delusional and almost certainly murderously criminal. And brutal. And unpredictable. And awful.

At that moment, Cosmos and Thor come up from the basement dungeon, both of them sporting bloodied faces.

Anita looks at Thor and bursts out laughing. It's not exactly the reaction I would have expected from someone seeing her romantic partner beaten up. I don't know how I feel about seeing Cosmos' face with his own blood trickling down it. When I was stuck in the trunk of his car, I wanted to punch him in the face myself. But I don't feel good seeing him hurt. I just feel uncomfortable and a little sad because he deserves people around him who don't punch him in the face over a disagreement about demons.

I cannot get out of here soon enough.

5

ryn has business with Cosmos. Presumably of the kind that doesn't involve having his face punched in again. Probably. Who knows. Apparently violent physical actions are unremarkable around here. This appears to be a cult of hyper-aggressive men and their unfortunately brainwashed female partners. I have no intention of becoming one of them. I'm leaving.

To my surprise, nobody actually stops me from walking out of the manor. I don't seem to be a prisoner here, at least, as far as everybody else is concerned.

The outside of the manor is as impressive as the exterior. These old English places are impressive. There's a particular mental and emotional weight to them that comes with their grim architecture. I should be used to old grim buildings by now, but Direview has a special ambiance all of its own.

I am wandering around out the front of the manor, not so much exploring so much as marinating in the unfortunate vibe of the place.

"Can I help you, madame?" The question comes from a refined but restrained looking man wearing an impeccably British brown suit. He doesn't look like anybody in particular. He looks like someone who could be anybody. A set of generic features sitting beneath coiffed hair.

"Who are you?"

"My name is Crichton. I am manservant to the gentlemen at Direview Manor. I am also available to tend to the needs of their respective ladies."

Okay, so his cards are on the table. He is in service to these psychopaths. Still, nothing ventured, nothing gained.

"I... uhm... I need to go to the airport. Or to a bus terminal leading to an airport. I need to go home. Can you direct me where you need to go?"

"I can take you, if you'd like, madame?"

"I would like. I would like very much, thank you."

I feel a sense of unparalleled relief as an opportunity to escape finally comes up. I don't mention that Cosmos wouldn't like this. I don't think that this man works for Cosmos, and I don't want to jinx things by invoking Cosmos' name. Look at me, already starting to think like a cultist. Invocation, what a concept. I cannot wait to get back to America.

. . .

C*osmos*

The house is quiet. After Bryn spent far too long taking up my time requiring briefing about the Fleisch affair, all I want to do is get back to Elise. Of course she's slipped away somewhere, which is very easy to do in Dire-view. This place was designed to allow everybody in it to have their own personal space. It is a very English design, and I used to be grateful for it, but now I mostly find myself annoyed by having to find Elise inside it. I know she has to still be here, because surely none of the others would let her get away. That would be a level of carelessness that I'm sure nobody present would indulge in.

I do end up finding Anita, the little demon Thor has taken pity on. My natural loathing for demons aside, I did promise to treat her like a person. The irony of that request seemed to be lost on everybody present.

Anyway, here we are.

"Where is Elise?"

Anita looks up from her embroidery. She's working on a sampler that appears to be a curse word. One that starts with C. She's like a little dark cloud of gloom. I imagine she makes Thor's life almost impossible.

"I don't know. I think I saw her talking to Crichton?"

"About?"

"Fuck if I know."

"Don't cross me, demon." My voice descends into a growl.

"Did you expect me to listen into every conversation in this place?" She gives me a look that I do not care for. Bryn has allowed all kinds of corruption into this house. Thor's female demon seems relatively harmless, preciously close to a house demon, but not quite.

"I know you did."

"What do I get if I tell you what you want to know?"

"I can tell you what you get if you don't tell me. A one-way trip to Hell."

"Kill joy," she sighs. "Fine. Crichton agreed to give her a ride to the bus stop."

"BRYN!" I leave the room shouting for the man who pretends to be in charge of this shit show. Bryn emerges from his office at my call, looking both concerned and annoyed.

"Crichton has absconded with my bride," I tell him.

"I am sure Crichton wouldn't help your wife escape Direview."

"Anita told me he drove her to the bus stop."

"I am certain Crichton wouldn't leave your wife at a bus stop. Don't worry. I am sure he knows what he is doing."

"She's my wife."

"Perhaps, but we are all charged with her protection."

Elise

"So your objection to Master Cosmos is because you believe that he, along with the rest of the inhabitants of Direview, are suffering under the unfortunate delusion that the world is inhabited by angels and demons?"

Crichton is making conversation with me in the car.

"Yes."

"I see."

Suddenly, there's a strange smell in the air. Sort of sulphurish. I wonder if he farted. I don't think he would do something like that, somehow. Crichton has the air of a man who has never passed gas in his life. I can't help myself. I sneak a glance over at him to see if he is truly the source of the stench.

Hot flames catch my eye and bring my attention all the way around to him. Crichton's head has been replaced with a flaming effigy of itself. His eyes are two burning coals stuck in a head that has no hair or skin, just a bone skull around which the flames lap and lick, somehow leaving his pristine brown suit completely alone.

I scream at the top of my lungs. I scream as though my very soul is being ripped out through my mouth.

"Terribly sorry, madam," Crichton says in that ineffable British accent of his. "It's ever so rude to smoke in the car."

He has returned to his typical appearance now, but I don't think I'll ever forget what I just saw, a living horror piloting a motor vehicle along the charming roads amidst the quaint English countryside.

"What the fuck are you!?"

"I believe you have some idea of that already." He is so very calm. He did this on purpose. He wanted to scare me. He has succeeded.

"You're a demon."

"Yes."

"No, you're fucking not."

"I believe I may be."

"What are you going to do to me?"

"Nothing at all, miss. I intend to take you to the bus stop, as you requested. After all, you are trapped in a world of delusion and must surely want to escape it immediately, returning to one where strangers break into your home in the dead of night and try to turn you into a blood sacrifice."

His passive-aggressive remarks are cutting in the extreme.

"Fine," I say. "Take me back to Direhall."

"Direview, madam."

"Whatever."

I am shaken to my core. I have to trust the evidence of my own eyes, don't I? Perhaps not. It might have simply been delusion, brought on by stress and suggestion. Yes. That's right. I'm not in a world full of demons. I'm insane. That's a much more comfortable conclusion, I think.

Cosmos is waiting for us as we approach the manor. This is the first time I have seen the place from a distance, and I have to say I am impressed and even awed by its raw Gothic charm. The place is like an ancient fortress, the sort of building that sparks imagination, much like Heidelberg Castle did, but in a more intense and darker way.

A flash of blue marks Cosmos' path as he paces back and forth at the wrought iron gates, sword in hand. I have no idea what he intends to do with that sword, but I do not think it is for me. Even at a distance he is impressively sexy.

"Oh dear," Crichton says calmly. "The master appears to be upset."

"I think you're in trouble," I say.

"I imagine we both are, though I agree, the sword is more likely intended for me than your good self."

Crichton brings the car to a halt at the gate. Cosmos is blocking the path, sword in hand. I'm not sure what he plans to do with it, given the car clearly doesn't belong to him. He's glaring at both of us. I think Crichton's original statement was correct. We are both in trouble.

"Shall I run him over?"

"What!? No!" I am shocked and horrified. Crichton merely smiles gently. I don't think he was ever serious, but who knows. He is a demon.

I groan internally as I realize that I have actually begun to accept it. It's absolute madness and yet here I am mentally considering demons as a reality I now need to contend with. Crichton's devilish plan has worked. He gained my trust, shocked me with a display, and now I am...

My thoughts are brutally interrupted as Cosmos puts his fist through the car window and drags Crichton out through the shattered glass. I find myself shrieking with panic at the notion that Crichton is about to be killed by my psychotic, self-assigned husband, but then I remember that he is a demon, and maybe he can't be killed. What are the rules surrounding supernatural staff?

I find myself clawing my way out the same window in the attempt to stop the attack. It's just a basic human reaction to protect a friend. I'm not exactly sure if Crichton qualifies as a friend. I don't have many friends. Okay, I don't have any friends. But he did offer to take me to the bus stop, and I think he would have done that if I'd wanted, demonic displays aside.

Cosmos has his sword held high in the air, poised to come down on the unfortunate Crichton. I scramble forward and over the butler, putting myself between Cosmos and the demon.

"Get out of the way, Elise."

"No. You're being stupid."

Those words do not improve his temper at all. He cuts his eyes at me, his expression one of pure fury. He wants to kill Crichton. He probably wants to take him apart the same way he gutted the unfortunate assassin who tried to come for me in the hotel room. I won't let that happen.

In the meantime, Bryn and Thor have both rushed out to save Crichton, but they needn't have bothered. The demon servant is more than capable of taking care of himself.

"Step aside, madam," Crichton says. He has risen to his feet and his voice is cool and calm. I do what Crichton says, and as I do, I see a flash of hurt pass over Cosmos' face. He doesn't like me taking orders from anybody else. But I don't want to be between a demon ready to fight and a demon slayer ready to slay.

Crichton lifts his hands to Cosmos. "I did not intend to cause your bride any harm, and I have not done her any, sir," he says. "Your quarrel is not with me, but with the burden a husband must bear. The fear of loss of the one he loves."

I thought for sure he was going to use his flaming head trick, but instead Crichton uses eloquence on Cosmos. It's super effective. Cosmos lowers the sword and extends an arm toward me. I go to him. Crichton has made me feel sorry for Cosmos, and that takes some work, especially when he's standing there, sword drawn, wild expression on his face.

He looks at me as I approach him and sees that my little journey through the broken car window was not without consequence. My hands have been cut in several places from the glass shards, and my knees didn't escape damage either.

"You're bleeding," Cosmos growls at me. "Why did you do something that stupid?"

"Why did I do something that stupid?" I shout at him as my temper flares. "I'm not the fucking moron who smashed glass everywhere for no reason. What did you think was going to happen? We were going to live in the car forever, me and Crichton, me toasting marshmallows on his demon head? We were going to get out. You were, as usual, an asshole."

Bryn looks thoroughly impressed. "This young lady is going to save me a lot in the way of breath if she keeps going that way."

Thor is smirking too.

I never expected to find allies here. I'm not surprised that these people find Cosmos nearly as impossible as I do. His recklessness is absolutely tedious.

He picks me up and carries me off inside. I don't think he liked having an audience. Anita is lurking by the front door as we go in. She gives me a little wave as I am carried over his shoulder. I give her a little wave back. A half hour ago I didn't want anything to do with these people, and now I am taking a lot of comfort from their combined presence.

He takes me to his room. The room I'm supposed to be sharing with him. With the bed we are supposed to also share as husband and wife. It certainly is large enough for more than two people, a massive four-poster construction. A fire burns in the grate of a ginormous fireplace. That should make the place feel luxurious and cozy, but all it really does is remind me of Crichton's head bursting into flame mid-drive.

My husband — if demons are real, I suppose that must be real too, carries me through to the ensuite bathroom. It is well furnished, but old. Direview has a slight air of ruin about it. It may be old and grand and Gothic, but it is not fully inhabited. How could it be? It is so large, and as far as I can tell, there are only three people living here, along with three demons.

Cosmos sets me down on the rim of a clawfoot tub and begins to look through the cabinet for medical supplies. He is not in a good mood, but it almost feels like his bad mood has nothing to do with me.

"You were, as usual, completely disobedient. Don't try to run from me, Elise. I will not tolerate you putting yourself in danger."

"But you will stuff me in a trunk and shatter glass all over a car I am in."

He sighs and almost seems to deflate. "I'm not good at being careful. I'm sorry."

C*osmos*

I have never had to be careful before. I am not sure I know how to be careful. It is so frustrating. All I want to do is protect Elise, but at every turn she makes it difficult for me to do that. And she is irritatingly adept at the art of argument, which means I feel on the back foot.

"You have to stop running away. I know this seems crazy, but I do not waste my time kidnapping and marrying random women just to drag them back here to this shit hole."

"I know."

I'm in the process of inspecting her hand for any remnants of broken glass — fortunately, the car windows have the kind of glass that turns into glass pebbles that still cut but don't gash the way most glass would.

"Wait. What? You know?"

"I can tell you don't like it here," she says. "The first thing that happened to you that I saw was Bryn putting you in a headlock. And they don't seem to mind listening to me tear strips off you."

"I'm sort of the black sheep," I admit. "Most of the Brotherhood are priests..."

"Brotherhood?"

"Did I not explain that part to you?"

She's shaking her head.

"I thought I had. But it has been a very long day. The Brotherhood is what we call our organization of demon hunters. A lot of us are priests. I'm not. I'm just a psychopath with a knife, as far as they're concerned."

"It's an easy mistake to make," she says with a little smirking grin.

She's giving me shit too, but it hits different coming from her.

"The good news is that your hand doesn't seem to be infiltrated with glass, and the cuts aren't that deep." I wrap a bandage around her hand and consider that fixed, for now. She'll be fine.

She yawns. I yawn too. This has been the definition of a fucking long day, and I think we're both ready to nap.

I pick her up and carry her to bed. This is our wedding night. It should be passionate and intense, but the moment we lie down, me feeling the weight of the day on my shoulders and eyelids, she not fighting me for once, sheer exhaustion sinks its claws into us both.

"I saw a demon," she whispers.

"What?"

"Crichton showed me his flaming demon head."

"Did he now."

"Yes. He seems nice, though. Are demons actually nice? Does that mean angels are actually secretly bad?"

"No," I mumble, snugging my arm around her waist. I don't want her going anywhere again. I'm too tired to chase her. That means pinning her down with me on the bed. She'll sleep whether she likes it or not.

E *lise*

He was sweet when he fixed my hand, and now, lying on the bed with him, I am surprised to find that I don't feel like wriggling out of his very possessive grasp. I thought I would want to be as far away from my rescuer cum abductor as possible, but my feelings toward Cosmos are surprisingly complex. I am angry at him and I feel a bit sorry for him. I'm grateful to him for rescuing me, and furious at how he went about it. Cosmos is one of the most flawed people I've ever met.

He is hot, though. And protective. And stubborn. Maybe as stubborn as I am. I am warm and I am safe. Before I know it, I am asleep.

6

Cosmos

"Master Cosmos! Get your boots off my coverlet at once!"

I open my eyes and discover Mrs Crocombe glowering down at me.

Elise is still with me. She's been woken up by Crocombe too and is squinting up at her. She looks adorable with her messy hair and slight air of confusion.

"Sorry. We were exhausted after a ten-hour drive," I say, swinging my feet off the bed.

"Hardly a proper wedding night," Crocombe huffs.

"Don't worry. We consummated our marriage in Germany."

"Cosmos!" Elise lets out a scandalized little gasp, which I enjoy immensely. She is such a proper thing, until she is angry, and then she is as feral as I am — almost.

"The two of you should shower and come down to breakfast," Crocombe says. She is not the kind to bring newlyweds breakfast in bed. She is the kind to barge in and complain they're not fucking. As much as a demon might try to pretend to be human, they always fail in the little things, the small social niceties and awarenesses that only real humans notice.

"We'll be down soon," I tell her. I don't mind the intrusion, because to me, being walked in on by a demon is as meaningful as being walked in on by a house cat.

Mrs Crocombe huffs her way out of the room. I turn over and look at Elise. "Good morning, wife."

"So this is real," she says in a half-wistful, half-confused tone. "It's all real. The marriage. The demons. The attempted murder."

I brush golden hair from her eyes. "They're all real. I am impressed. Yesterday you were absolutely refusing to believe any of it. Today you are willing to accept it all."

"That's because science is about collecting data. The multiple murder attempts and the flaming skull butler were convincing. I've always been able to trust my senses. So far, the evidence points toward it all being true. Heinously, bizarrely true. I wonder if the part about the resurrection is true too."

"Fleisch is an end times death cult."

"They're scientists. Geneticists. Undertaking the strangest and perhaps most significant project in recent history. Trying to use the blood of humans of certain lineages to somehow animate the flesh of a Nazarene. Fascinating."

"Not fascinating," I chastise her. "Mad, and dangerous. The return of the Lord might have been prophesied, but it also means the end of the world is nigh. For everybody to keep living their lives, we want the divine to stay firmly on their side of the playing table."

I don't think I've convinced her. I think I've intrigued her.

"They would use you as a blood slave and then kill you as a sacrifice."

"Maybe. But imagine the data. If I could get into that laboratory you keep talking about, the things I could see..."

I grab her and throw her over onto her stomach. She's going to be spanked long and hard for even teasing about getting into league with Fleisch.

"They are the enemy. They are a direct danger to you. And they are not to be considered anything other than the murderous maniacs they are. Do you understand?"

I expect a gasp or a wail of contrition. Instead, I hear a moan. She has the nerve to enjoy this, little minx. She likes pain. She thrives on it. Does she know how much I enjoy imparting it? How hard my cock is every time my palm falls on her ass? No. She's too busy trying not to make it obvious in the way her hips writhe and dance for me. Elise is a liar, though she'd never admit it. Not even to herself. I could shame her badly if I wanted. I could point out her wetness and the scent she is emitting. I could make her confront her need. For now I let her keep her sexy little lies. I spank her longer than I intended to, and harder than I intended to at first. She can take so much more punishment than her tender frame would suggest.

Her knuckles whiten as she grips the sheets. She's grinding herself against the bed, pretending not to be utterly turned on by this treatment. Elise is a bad girl hiding inside a good girl. I intend to stoke this fire in her. I will punish her, and she will mistake it for real discipline, but in truth I will be bringing out the devil in my little angel.

Every time my palm lands, she moans. And every time she moans, my cock gets harder and more impossible to ignore. Being with Elise is an exercise in self-control. I want to be inside her always. I want to feel her tight, angelic walls gripping my cock and anointing it with the juices of her need.

"Bad girl," I growl. "I think you like this. I think you love being thrashed."

She doesn't deny it, but how could she. I am spreading her legs and finding that pink chalice waiting for me with pouting lips. She's soaked, just as I knew she would be. We may be strangers, Elise and I, but our bodies react as if we have known one another for a very long time. We fit.

The sight of the head of my cock at the aperture of those tender pink lips is enough to make my balls tighten. Elise is holding her breath, gripping the bedding, her thighs tense as she tries to hold herself perfectly still for me. There is one of those eternal moments as I slide into her, her lips spreading in that lewd way they must to allow me inside. I pause, feeling the heat of her interior before me, the tight grip of her pussy just taking hold of me. I hold myself there a few moments longer, letting her feel this deep connection before driving deep all the way inside her, her hot depths engulfing me.

Fucking Elise is like touching heaven. There is redemption in her cunt, and in the pleasure we share. She's arching up toward me, her pink ass bearing my palm prints. Every time her hips grind, she grips me tighter, her inner walls doing their best to milk me into her cunt. Holding back is almost more than I can bear, but I still have the faint memory of this being a punishment of sorts. I am teaching her what is and what is not correct. Obeying me will make her a good girl; being drawn to the darkness of those who wish for her destruction will make her a candidate for discipline.

Pulling almost all the way out of her, I spank her again, hard slaps going from cheek to cheek, relighting the fire I set earlier. I want to hear her whimper, but all she does is moan and grip my cock with that hungry pussy.

"You're mine," I remind her. "And you are protected by the Brotherhood. Fleisch are the enemy. Repeat that back."

When she doesn't immediately obey, I pull my cock all the way out of her pussy and aim fresh slaps, no longer at her cheeks, but at her soaked cunt. My fingers catch those soft, swollen lips and draw forth cries from her. God, I love the way she cries.

"I'm yours!" She pants the words breathily and that is all I need to hear to be compelled to sink myself back inside her and make that deeply true. I need my seed to soak her pussy. I need her to drip with my essence. I need for her to be a little bit me and entirely mine, now and forever.

E*lise*

Holy fuck does this man undo me. He makes everything that is crazy, sane. And he makes everything I thought I knew evaporate in the force of his lust.

Orgasm leaves my body relaxed and my mind clear. Clear enough for questions to begin to infiltrate. Logical questions. I already half-despair that there is next to no chance at having them answered. Cosmos doesn't exist in the same world I do. His priorities are so different.

"What is wrong, angel?" He brushes his teeth gently over my shoulder, the way a sane man might use his lips. Cosmos always has edge, even when he is tender.

"I'm wondering what happens now. Do you want me to live here in this old manor, with your friends and their wives?"

Cosmos looks momentarily confused. I don't think he actually thought this far ahead. When you start a relationship with a marriage, there's not a lot of places to go. We've begun at the end of romance, and now we're trying to reverse engineer our way into something real.

"Well, I was going to keep being a demon slayer, and I figured you could..."

"What? Be barefoot and pregnant?"

"Absolutely not!" He looks scandalized.

"Oh. Right. Of course. You had a vasectomy. So you want me to leave my job, sit in England, and rot into my old age?"

"No," he frowns. "I'm going to train you as a demon hunter."

"You're going to... what now? What makes you think I'm capable of hunting demons? I'm a scientist. I'm a female scientist with no ability with weaponry, or..."

"Shhhhh..." He presses a finger to my lips. "I will find something for you to do. You may not necessarily dispatch demons yourself. You may track them via data. Doesn't that sound like fun?"

The truly twisted, kinky, absolutely fucked up thing is that it does sound like fun.

"How would that work?"

He sits up, his tattooed torso an immediate distraction. "Let me show you something. It's a place sorely underutilized at Direview. Bryn is too busy with parish work, and Thor — I don't even know what Thor does most of the time. But this place was actually built to do the job they forget to do these days. Come on. It's upstairs."

Tucked away at the upper corner of Direview, there is a room with a green door. It looks very different from the other doors, which are wood-toned in keeping with the rest of the old aesthetic. This one is wooden too, but someone took paint to it, tried to mark it as being special and apart from the rest of the place. It has been left to get covered in dust, almost like the demon servants don't want to touch it. I am even more intrigued now.

"Why is this so much more dilapidated than every other dilapidated thing here?"

"Direview has had a cash flow problem for some time now. Bryn wouldn't know how to make money if you gave him a lemonade stand. Thor's barely a person. Demons don't care about money as much as you'd think they would. Everything that stands here stand because of the brothers who don't live here."

I am listening to him until he unlocks the door with a little brass key. The door swings open. I expect to hear the creak of rusted hinges, but it opens smoothly and silently.

Every single window in this room is blacked out, but it is brightly lit by a verdant hue. The feeling I get stepping into this room is almost mystical. It's like coming home to a home I'd forgotten I had.

I love a bank of computers more than I love almost anything. This is impressive. Very impressive. This draws me in, the glow of at least two dozen screens shining their data on me.

The tech is old. These aren't flat screens. These are CRT monitors with blocky green text and big, thick cursors blinking at me. There are no nice WYSIWYG (what you see is what you get) interfaces displaying the information in cheerful charts and with bold text. There's just the data. Beautiful data.

"What does this refer to?"

"Most of the upper echelons of governments around the world run on outdated technology. Well, most may be an exaggeration, but you'd be shocked how many government systems are run on early DOS platforms to this day. This bank of computers is linked to several international systems with access to older satellites. It's not the best data. It needs to be interpreted and…"

I'm not listening. I'm sitting down in the older style office chair, low backed and covered in beige corduroy. Arm rests far too thin to provide any real resting potential. Lumbar support practically nonexistent. It feels correct.

The keyboard clacks when I touch it. It, like everything else, is incredibly dated. I bet if I pick up the mouse… yes. It has an actual physical ball rolling around inside it to function as a tracker.

"This is amazing," I breathe. "Is there documentation?"

"Here," he says, lifting the lid of a box full of printer paper. Not modern printer paper, all in separate sheets, but proper printer paper, the kind that has perforated edges with little holes in it the gears of the printer fit through so it moves through the mechanism at the right rate. And on this paper are endless screeds of information and documentation.

"Okay," I say. "You've got me."

"This until lunch time," he says. "After lunch, we work out and I start teaching you how to defend yourself."

"Uh huh."

I am not listening. I am reading. I am happy.

7

E *lise*

This is truly fascinating, and actually much more in-depth than I imagined it would be. Working with limited tech means being creative. I've already formulated a potential way to cross-reference various streams to…

"Right. Time you ate."

I am rudely interrupted by my husband of all of two days who has not yet learned how dangerous it is to interrupt me while I am concentrating.

"Hey!" I exclaim as Cosmos lifts me bodily out of the chair. "I just got started."

He shakes his head at me. "You've been at this for five hours straight. It's time to eat."

"What!? No. I need to work. You said I had until lunch time!"

"It is almost three o'clock. I came in twice and you didn't even know I was here," he says reprovingly. "You're done working. It's time to eat."

He's carrying me back through the halls of Direview. I am mad. I didn't get a chance to save where I was. I was halfway through a thought and that thought is probably going to dangle the entire time I'm trying to eat, only to disappear the second I reach for it once I'm allowed back to work.

"Put me down! I need to make some notes."

"I will not put you down. Crocombe has made you something to eat, and you are going to eat it. Trust me, you do not want to cross a house demon who has gone out of her way to feed you."

The dining room at Direview is designed to hold far more people than Cosmos and me. The two of us sit at one end, him at the head, me at his right-hand side. Mrs Crocombe has made a pie, a meat infested pastry casing. I am not hungry.

Cosmos seems to like it. He eats, while I sit and try to think of some way back to the computer. I don't want him to notice that I'm not eating, so I distract him with questions.

"So what's your deal? Who's your dad? Your mom? Where do you come from?"

"My mother was Korean. She died giving birth to me. My father was an American soldier. He brought me back from Korea when his tour there ended and raised me in half a dozen army bases. He didn't have much time for a kid. I got into a lot of trouble. That's where I found religion." He gives me the Cliff notes version. I appreciate that, though it makes me curious. I really don't know my husband at all. It's not really my fault. It's just that's what happens when you're forced into a wedding of dubious legality in the middle of the night.

"Would have thought you'd have joined the military?"

"They didn't think I was temperamentally suited," he says with a little smirk. "I was a bad kid. One of the ones they worry about in kindergarten. It's just how I've always been. A little more aggressive than most, a little bit more physical than most, a lot more interested in knives..." He smiles ruefully, reflecting what I imagine is a life of trying to pretend to be normal, all the while knowing he was never going to fit in. "But the church takes what the war machine won't. One of the old Brotherhood found me before I got myself thrown into jail and helped me channel my violent tendencies toward demons instead of people. These guys accept me for what I am. They make me useful, instead of a liability."

"And what happened to your dad?"

"He's still around," Cosmos says. "He was recruited into some top-level government gang bang around the time I was recruited into this place. We don't talk much. He's always in some exotic country, doing something unspeakable."

"Like father, like son," I quip.

"I guess, yeah," Cosmos agrees.

"He probably saved hundreds, if not thousands of lives. The Brotherhood guy, I mean."

"Probably," he agrees. "I owe a lot to the Brotherhood. They gave me what my own family could not, and what the world would not. That's why I still serve, even when I disagree with the new regime."

"You mean Bryn."

"Yes," he says. "I mean Bryn."

The food isn't bad, but I'm really not hungry. I do like learning about Cosmos, though. And I've found a way to keep those ideas I had close. The thread of my thoughts doesn't have to dangle anymore. I can jot them down while we talk, in a medium that's not going anywhere anytime soon.

C osmos

She thinks I can't see her scratching her little notes into the side of the table. Bryn wouldn't like that, which is precisely why I let her keep doing it. I can also see she's pushed her pie around a lot more than eaten it. She is a very disobedient little angel.

I have never looked after anybody before. I'm not sure that I know how to do it. Should I be lecturing her about eating her food and keeping her pen to herself? Or should I follow my natural chaotic live-and-let-live instincts and say nothing?

As it turns out, Mrs Crocombe is going to do some of the intervention all on her own. She comes out to see how her meal has been received and is not well pleased to see that my angel has turned her nose up at it.

"You don't like the food?"

"The food's lovely. I don't have much appetite, that's all."

"Newlywed nerves," Mrs Crocombe says, sympathetic. "I should have made you something lighter. Something with chicken, and perhaps rice. You seem to be the jittery type if you don't mind me saying."

"You can say what you like," Elise says. A silent, unspoken sentence follows, one that tells everybody that she doesn't care what anybody else says. She's got a natural arrogance and strong-headedness I find very appealing.

Mrs Crocombe clears the table

"Can I go now?" Elise is halfway out of her chair as she asks the question. She's so impatient.

"No. We need to work out."

"Ugh. No," she sighs. "My strengths are indoor-based. Sitting down. I'm not a working out sort of person."

She's walking toward the door, as if she intends to go back to the office without my permission. I sit back in my chair, watching her defy me and planning the punishment that will be hers.

Bryn happens to walk in at that moment. He nods at Elise and smiles. He approves of her. She's a bookish angel who doesn't seem to cause any kind of trouble as far as he knows. He thinks she's my victim, snatched from her life against her will and installed in the trunk of the car. She hasn't even tried and she's already got him wrapped around her little finger.

"Hello, Elise," he says.

"Hello, Father Bryn," she replies, sweet as pie.

"How are you feeling today?"

"Very good. I have discovered the computers you have upstairs, thanks to Cosmos. I'm learning to run demon analysis."

"Very impressive," Bryn says with a slightly patronizing tone that is not lost on Elise. I see her eyes narrow slightly, and then a fixed smile establishes itself on her face. I wonder how many times she has used this expression before in her professional life while older men praise her for knowing what a computer is.

Bryn doesn't notice, because Bryn has already noticed something else. Direview is his ancestral home, and though it may be the seat of the Brotherhood, it is also fully furnished with items belonging entirely to him. That means the fancy long table is his. And so is the equation Elise scratched into it with the tip of her fork not long ago.

He storms over to the table and gives me a furious look, as if I might have developed a taste for scrawling numbers and symbols.

"What the bloody hell happened here?"

Surely, he already knows. Who else would scrawl mathematical notation into the side of a table besides Elise?

"I think it's time we worked out," Elise says quickly. "Got to get those reps in before we atrophy."

"Yes," I agree. "Time to work out. We'll be in the dungeon if you need us, Bryn."

"Crichton better be able to fix this," he growls. "Or I'll take it out on you, Cosmos."

I stand up and walk over to Elise, draping my arm over her shoulders. "You're welcome to try," I smile.

E*lise*

Bryn is quite dangerous looking when he's angry. There's something perpetually smoldering about him that concerns me. It's a different kind of danger than you get with Cosmos. It's not the kind that dismembers a man alive in a hotel room for daring to try to hurt his wife. It's the kind that remembers a slight for years, perhaps even generations, before eventually and inexorably seeking revenge. And there's something else too. Something that I shudder to call mystical, but it is there.

I look up at Bryn, feeling quite guilty for having ruined his property. I thought I was rebelling against Cosmos, but I guess I was just being destructive, and when you're destructive there's really no end of consequences.

"I'm sorry," I say. "It was my fault. I'll pay to repair it."

"And how will you repair a table from the Elizabethan era?"

"Uhmm..."

I glance up at Cosmos, who does not seem to give even a fraction of a shit.

"If you were my wife, I'd be spanking you over that table," Bryn says. "Sparing the lash spoils the bride, Cosmos."

"She's not your wife, and if you put a finger on her, I will show you the inside of your belly," Cosmos speaks casually, but entirely seriously.

"Which is why I told you that I hold you responsible." Bryn nails Cosmos with a dark stare, then turns his gaze back to me. "I'd hoped you'd be a fine addition to Direview, Elise. I think you still can be. Do not allow your husband to be a bad influence."

With that, Bryn stalks out, leaving us in the miasma of his tall, dark, and brooding presence.

We both let out a long breath when we're certain he's gone.

"I'm sorry I got you into trouble."

"Oh, don't worry about Bryn. I don't care what he thinks."

"Maybe you should, if he is your boss."

"He's not my boss. He just happens to have slid out between the right pair of legs. Let's go. You need to be able to protect yourself. I might not always be here to stop you from getting what you deserve."

He takes me out through the kitchen, down to the basement. I didn't expect it to be as well-appointed and fresh looking as it is. It's been renovated and modernized in a way that sets it very much apart from the rest of Direview. The doors down here are modern, and the flooring has been made nice and even. There are weapons all over the walls, and in one area there are mats down, the kind of mats you can fall on and not take any real damage. This is not my kind of scene.

Cosmos strips his shirt off.

Maybe this is my kind of scene.

Simple lust has taken me a very long way over the last couple of days. I have made some seriously bad decisions and allowed some very terrible things to happen to me. Right now I am not thinking about anything close to exercise. Well, maybe it is a little close. Cosmos is sinfully hot. His body isn't just exercise fit. It's killer fit. Literally. The things he's capable of doing are absolutely unspeakable. Occasionally, my mind flashes back to that bloody hotel room, reminding me what he's capable of. Most of the time he seems rakish and relaxed, but true darkness runs in his veins. I can't forget that.

"We need to get you some workout clothes," he says, suddenly realizing that I am not at all dressed for the occasion. "Today you can watch me. Tomorrow, you start working out yourself."

If he'd just said that in the beginning, I wouldn't have resisted. Watching Cosmos move is a pleasure all its own, a kind of foreplay that makes me tingle with anticipation. He moves like a serpent through a series of martial arts dances — that's probably not the word for them, but they are like dances. His body his muscular yet lithe, he's not overburdened with bulk. From the rippling plane of his abdomen to his firm ass, everything about him is engineered for what he is doing right now: practicing death and turning me the fuck on.

"Tell you what," he says, stopping for a second. A few dark strands of hair are hanging in his eyes. He looks like a character out of a sweaty anime. "Just go and ask one of the girls if they have something to wear."

I feel very awkward asking that question, but it gets me out of the immediate imperative to exercise in any way. I find Nina and Anita in the kitchen, again. The entirety of Direview may as well be the kitchen as far as they are concerned.

"So, I hate to do this, but Cosmos wanted me to ask you for gym clothes, but I'm not going to do that. I will, however, have some of those scones."

"Girls' trip!" Nina beams. "We'll all go into Direford and go shopping. It's been so long since we were out."

"I don't think that's a good idea," Anita says, uncomfortably. "They still think I'm a murderer there."

"Oh. Right. London, then."

"They're never going to let us go to London on our own."

"And why not? We're all grown women. And Elise needs something decent to wear."

Anita shakes her head. "Bryn isn't going to let you out of his sight, Nina. He's terrified of Fleisch, and Thor doesn't trust me as far as he can throw me."

"We can take Crichton with us. He'll look after us."

"Three girls and a demon," Anita grins. "Roadtrip!"

"No, Nina."

I've gone with the other girls to ask for permission to go to London. I think it's ridiculous that we've all been reduced to this. Grown women shouldn't be going around asking their husbands and male protectors for permission to leave the house. Not in England, or America, or anywhere civilized.

Nina has asked very nicely. But Bryn doesn't even look up from his paperwork as he summarily refuses to let her have the most basic human rights.

"We want to go shopping. We need to go shopping," Nina tries again. "Elise is practically living in a lab coat, and Anita hardly has any clothes that don't make her look like a goth, and I wouldn't mind updating my wardrobe."

"No, Nina."

"Alright, let me put it another way," Nina says, pushing her pretty red hair back from her face. "I am going shopping with Anita and Elise and you're going to give me some money to do it."

Bryn stops writing and puts down his pen. I notice that Anita has taken a step back, as if she's afraid. I stay where I am, watching the way Bryn's dark eyes lock onto his wife.

"I think you know better than to speak to me that way, Nina," he says. His eyes flicker to Anita and me. "If you ladies will excuse us, I need to have a discussion with my wife."

Anita grips my sleeve and pulls me out of the room. Nina hasn't moved. She looks very proud and elegant, her chin raised, her green eyes lit with determination.

"We're not going to London, are we?"

I murmur the question to Anita as we shut Bryn's door behind us. Anita obeys Bryn. I wonder if that is because she identifies herself as a demon, and Bryn is a demon slayer. There is so much madness in this big, rambling old house.

Anita leans up against the wall and shrugs. She's taking this in stride, but as the sound of leather making contact with flesh starts to emanate through the door, I can't be as calm. Bryn is punishing Nina for daring to ask him to go out. One crack after another comes through the door, and after a half-dozen of those strokes, I start to hear Nina gasp and whimper.

"She didn't do anything wrong. Why is he punishing her?"

"Because he's a kinky fucker," Anita smirks. She's not upset by what she's hearing. If anything she looks amused by it. I don't have her equanimity. Hearing someone being hurt for no good reason makes me very upset. I stand, staring at the door, my fists clenched. When a particularly loud squeal can be heard, I put my hand on the handle.

"Don't," Anita says. "She wouldn't want you to interfere."

"So we just let each other get beaten? Is that it? We're all submissive little whipping girls waiting for our masters to thrash us?"

"When you say it that way it sounds kind of hot," Anita grins. She's irrepressible, and quite demonic. I don't share her amusement or her joy. I am appalled. And I am once more propelled to action.

I am in our room, packing my bag. I don't have many things left to pack, but I am packing them, nonetheless.

Cosmos comes in and puts his hand on my shoulders, leaning over me to look at the pitiful bag of possessions.

"What are you doing? I thought I asked you to get some gym clothes, not pack everything you own."

"I'm leaving."

I expect him to come over all authoritarian and tell me that I'm not going to leave, that I'm his wife and I'll do as he says. But he surprises me by asking a question instead.

"Why?"

"Because this is a house full of controlling misogynists, and I am not interested in living here for another day. Did you know Bryn whips Nina if she dares leave the house? We just asked to go to London and she's…" I draw in a breath.

"Bryn's a pretty intense disciplinarian," Cosmos says. "But we can go to London, you and I."

"And what about Nina? She's stuck with that man. He has to be twice her age. There's something so fucked up there."

"There's a lot of fucked up there," Cosmos agrees. "But Nina chose to marry him, knowing what he was."

"Did she? Or was it like our wedding? She barely knew what was happening and just ended up in wedlock basically by accident?"

"There are no accidents. And no, they were married in the traditional way. They're in love, as strange as that might seem to you and me. I'm sure Nina knew what she was going to get when she went and confronted Bryn. You and I can go to London. Let's go now."

I hesitate.

"I feel bad leaving the others. Anita and Nina wanted to go."

"Well, there's no chance Thor or Bryn would allow them to go with me. They don't trust me with anything. They certainly wouldn't trust me with their wives."

I frown. "Why are you the black sheep of this fucked-up family? You seem to do more than they do."

"It's precisely because I do things that I'm the black sheep. They usually don't approve of the way I behave. But I do what needs to be done. And what needs to be done right now, is you need to be taken on a shopping trip."

Holy shit. I think I love him.

Not because of the shopping. Because he wants to make me happy. Bryn's first instinct was to tell Nina no. Cosmos' first instinct is to tell me yes. I think I have the pick of the bunch. Cosmos is hotter and sweeter than any man I have ever met.

He offers me his hand and draws me down the hall, away from my half-packed bag and to the outside. He seems to have an instinct for what I need. He's dominant, but he's not controlling the way Bryn seems to be.

On the way out, we pass Anita, who is skulking like a dark shadow in Direview's halls. I feel sorry for her. I don't know why. I suppose she's a fellow captive. There's something lost about her.

"Anita, do you want to come shopping? Cosmos is taking us."

"Let me ask Thor," she says before smirking. "Just kidding."

"Where's Nina? You think she'd want to come?"

"I'm sure she'd want to come, but she and Bryn disappeared into their room and haven't emerged since. So I guess it's you and me and Cosmos. Wait. Does that make me a third wheel? I don't want to third wheel. Maybe the two of you should go. Enjoy the romance."

"Where's your romance?"

Anita shrugs. "Thor's around somewhere. Don't worry about me. It's sweet of you to think about me, but I don't need to shop right now. Have fun in town."

"She's sweet, for a demon," Cosmos says as we leave Direview.

"I like her."

"Good. It's good to make friends. And there are hardly any people who understand what being part of the Brotherhood is like. It's a strange world, running parallel with what most people call the real world. You've had a taste of it so far, but it runs deep. Nina's an innocent to it all. But Anita, aside from being a demon, she might be able to provide some deeper insight."

I like that he's willing to change his opinion. When he first met Anita, he was ready to slay her. Now he's telling me to make friends with her if I like. Flexibility doesn't seem to be one of the core tenets of this cult There's some hope for Cosmos yet.

We drive down to the village. It's not London, but it's something. There aren't a lot of shops down there, but there is a chain store or two with generic clothes, and that's all I need. Some pants, some skirts, some tops, some workout clothes.

I've never been much of a shopper. I find myself kind of nervous as I walk the racks with Cosmos not all that far behind me.

He dresses very well, and what I'm picking out feels sort of... I don't know. Basic? I frown to myself in the changing room mirror and decide that maybe I'll be more adventurous, like Anita is and like Cosmos is. They both have an edge to them that makes me wonder if those two aren't a better fit than him and me.

I emerge wearing slacks and a beige sweater.

"What?" I ask the question, noticing a strange expression on his face. He must think I am such a nerd. He's probably wondering why he picked me up. Oh right, the alleged angel blood. That's delusional.

"You're beautiful," he says.

I blush and try not to smile too broadly. I like him liking me. Out here in plain public, we're an odd couple. But in his eyes, I'm beautiful. I don't know why. But I know that he's not a liar.

"Thank you," I whisper.

He takes me by my hands and draws me back into the changing room, closing the curtain behind us. "I want to make you happy, Elise. I know we're still strangers to one another. And I know I'm not exactly husband material. But if you'll have me, I'll make you happy."

I stare into his face. I can't believe a man like this is making these vows to me. He's so much more... everything than I ever thought I'd have.

"I'm not an angel," I tell him. "I'm just a woman. And I'm going to disappoint you in the end because I'm not an angel. I'm a scientist."

"You're my angel," he tells me, cupping my face in his hands.

My heart is breaking, because I know that all his desire for me is based on a delusion. Yes, I saw Crichton's head turn to fire, and maybe I have to admit the existence of demons. Fine. But it's still an incredible stretch to imagine that there is anything special or angelic about me.

"Excuse me, sir, madam, only one person can be in the changing rooms at one time."

An English woman has come to kick us out of the store, but not before I get some sensible, comfortable clothing to wear. Cosmos doesn't make any trouble, but I see the reckless grin he flashes her as we leave, and her answering blush. He's sexual dynamite. He could have any woman he wanted. It's going to really hurt when he realizes that he doesn't want me after all.

"Don't sulk," he says. "You're far too classy to be fucked in a changing room, anyway, aren't you?"

I find myself grinning. Yes. I am far too classy... or I thought I was.

He takes me out to the car, having paid for everything I picked out. I've never been treated by a man this way. I've always looked after myself completely. It feels nice in some ways, but terrifying in others. I feel warm at the idea Cosmos wants to look after me but scared at the notion I am dependent on him now.

"My mom's bills... if they're not paid..."

"Don't worry," he says. "I have already organized it. You can call your mom tomorrow and talk to her. I'm not keeping you as a prisoner. I'm trying to take care of you and yours, and I hope that you'll realize it is safer this way."

"Nothing that relies on anybody else to do anything is safe," I say, almost reflexively.

He leans over and kisses my cheek, a simple and sweet expression of reassurance. It is so hard to reconcile this romantic with the man who stuffed me into the trunk of the car just yesterday. I have to get a grip and remember that this man is dangerous. Very dangerous. And no amount of beige sweaters and sweet nothings will change that.

"I promised Crocombe we'd be back at Direview in time for tea," he says. "We're having a welcome dinner for you."

That sounds sweet. They're trying. But what underlies their trying is dark, and I'm not going to fall for it. I can't forget that I am missing work, that my apartment is a bloody mess, and that there's probably going to be a missing person alert for me — unless Cosmos' associates have cleaned my life up behind me, just rolled it up like a carpet.

I'm caught between two urges, one to escape and one to just sink into this world that is being made for me. The latter urge terrifies me. There is something so seductive about not having to try anymore, not having to make choices anymore, just being able to do as I am told and be a kept woman in a dark world.

8

"Welcome to our little family, Elise." Bryn toasts me with a crystal glass full of port or maybe blood. Who knows with this collective of the terminally odd.

Dinner at Direview is held in the main hall with everybody present. Each of the men sits on one side of the table, and their respective partners sit on the other side. The exception, of course, is Bryn, who insists on sitting at the head of the table like the tall, dark, dominating figurehead he is. Nina sits at the other end of the table, and the rest of us are spaced out in a way I think is kind of awkward but what do I know. The food is good, and I am glad for it because it gives me an excuse not to say anything.

Conversation goes on around me and over me. Nina makes a few polite attempts to draw me out, and I keep my responses short and polite in return. I am tired. I am scared. For a time I managed to enjoy the data center upstairs but now that I am surrounded by the people of Direview it's not possible to ignore the cult vibes in this ancient dining room.

I find myself staring at Thor out of the corner of my eye. I don't know where to place him in this mess, because aside from looking like a massive beast of a man, he seems somewhat normal. I'm curious about so many things, caught between just the slightest hint of belief because I saw Crichton's flaming head trick, and the more concrete certainty that none of this could possibly be real.

Finally, the meal is at an end. I've managed to avoid being drawn into real conversation, which suits me fine.

"Why don't the ladies enjoy the drawing room while we discuss business?"

I roll my eyes at Bryn's misogyny, but everybody else agrees and so I go along with it. I do wonder what business the three men have to talk about. What do mad cultists with demonic slaves and brainwashed brides chat about after dinner?

"So," Nina says, settling into a chaise lounge like the elegant, willowy angel she is. "What's your angel power?"

"I have no idea what an angel power is." I try not to sound completely derisive as I answer, and I'm not sure I entirely succeed. Angel power sounds like a special kind of absolute bullshit.

"I have the ability to enter the mist and see things that never were. It's kind of like being psychic with extra steps."

"I don't have any powers," I shrug. "I don't believe in powers."

"I am sure you have some kind of as yet untapped ability. Perhaps it will emerge under stress."

"Two different men tried to kill me in the same day, and no special powers emerged. I respect your beliefs, but I don't believe them. I know there are demons, but I'm not sure there's such a thing as angels. I've yet to see any other evidence.

Anita and Nina exchange smug little smiles. "It's okay," Anita says. "I would have thought this was all bullshit too until it got weird. When things get strange for you, you can talk to us. Don't be ashamed."

"Thanks," I say. They mean well, I think. They're just all absolutely off their heads with ideologies. "I'm not ashamed."

"Good," Anita smiles. She truly does not give a fraction of a fuck. I find her more relatable than most here. It seems to me that there's a possibility she could be an ally. Nina is too head over heels for Bryn and too legitimately convinced that she's an angel.

There's a kind of awkward silence, in which it seems to occur to us all at the same time that we have nothing in common besides being the bedmates of the men who are discussing business in another room.

"What's the plan here," I ask, breaking the silence. "Do you have plans for your lives, or..."

"Well, I'm technically sort of wanted for murder," Anita says. "So I keep a low profile."

"I'm happy at the moment with how things are," Nina replies. "It's nice to finally be able to rest somewhere and call it home."

"So Bryn and Thor aren't trying to turn you two into demon slayers?"

"No!" Anita laughs. "Thor's had enough of me slaying things to last a lifetime, and Bryn wouldn't stand for Nina being in anything that looked like danger."

"He's very protective," Nina agrees.

"There's a computer bank upstairs that I'm using to track demonic activity," I say. "Cosmos is going to teach me how to slay them."

The girls are interested in that revelation, especially Anita. "Is it wrong if I also want to slay demons? I am a demon, so I suppose it would be batting against my own team. It's strange how many demons there are in an anti-demon organization."

"Very strange," I agree.

"I think you'll feel better when you discover what your angel power is," Nina insists. "Maybe we can help you find it."

"Maybe Crichton can help her. Crichton showed me Hell. And he saved me from it. He really doesn't get enough credit. Let's call him," Anita suggests.

Crichton appears once summoned. Via bell, not by an arcane ceremony.

"How may I help you ladies?"

He's so easy to ignore. He has such a plastic face; not plastic like the material, plastic in the way his features are always generic and never quite the same. I wonder if he's still the same man I met on the first day here, or if his demon features mean nobody will ever really know what he looks like. I can't work out why a demon would sit around serving humans tea and scones, and occasionally frightening the hell out of the odd girl who fails to properly believe in things that catch fire in the head. I find myself staring at him with more curiosity than ever.

But it's Nina who has the question.

"Crichton, how can Elise find her angel powers?"

His expression remains impassive. "I believe what you are describing is a manifestation of the divine, and it cannot be predicted."

"So you don't know?" Nina sounds very disappointed.

"Nobody knows. Nobody can know. Manifestations of angelic power are not chosen or handed out like perks. They're rare, even among those of the blood. Merely having angelic parentage does not guarantee that one is special. A child born to two geniuses might only be of average intelligence. A child born of an angel might be merely human."

"Oh." Nina's face falls. She was really hoping I'd be able to make rainbows come out of my ass or similar, I think. I feel a little bad for her. I think she's lonely. She wants someone like her to relate to, but that's not going to happen.

"That's okay," I say. "I have a pretty nice life as a normal human anyway. Or I did, before I was attacked and kidnapped and made to leave my life behind."

There's another one of those awkward silences.

Crichton smiles patiently. "Very few brides have come to Direview of their own accord, and many have been unhappy here."

"But?"

"Oh. There's no but," he says. "I tell the truth. I believe it is the least you deserve."

Anita lets out a snorting laugh. "Yeah, you're not going to get any uplifting words of comfort from Crichton."

This is all so very British.

"Maybe I could have something to drink. Something strong."

"A brandy, perhaps, madame?"

"Yes. Whatever. Perfect."

A glass of amber liquid is delivered into my hand. I drink deeply and follow that with a deep breath. Neither one of those things really helps. What I am trying to de-stress about can't be solved with a little alcohol and breathing exercises.

"My mother escaped Direview," Nina says solemnly. "But she never really got away. And in the end, here I am. This place inexorably draws the people who are meant to be here."

"Because of some angel who couldn't keep his celestial dick in his pants?" I say. "Let's say that's real and true. Even if it was, why should it decide our lives? So what if you're a little bit angel, or demon, or just plain human? You should be able to live the life you choose, not spend it in this rotting old place. The world is out there, not in here."

"Yeah!" Anita fist pumps my statement. Nina looks a little more reserved.

"It's not as easy as you think. There are forces of evil..."

"Of course. There are always forces of evil. That doesn't mean you let yourself be turned into a prisoner."

Crichton is still here, listening with a quiet smile. The alcohol has made me feel more brave and forthright than before. I hold the tumbler out to Crichton, indicating I am ready for more. He obliges by refilling my glass once, twice, three times. I don't usually drink. I don't usually need to.

Nina and Anita are discussing something or other about stuff and perhaps things. My mind is full of recursive thoughts that have only one possible conclusion: something must be done. These dark misogynists must be confronted.

"Where are you going?" Nina asks the question as I wobble my way toward the door.

"Who cares, I'm following," Anita declares.

I have a little entourage of the confused, concerned, and amused behind me as I stalk the halls of Direview like a vengeful spirit, though one that actually exists because I am real and they are not.

"THERE'S NO SUCH THING AS GHOSTS!"

I make my thesis statement as I roll through the door somewhat sideways. I meant to open it but I find my shoulder making contact first and then I just sort of go with the motion, spinning myself into the midst of the Brotherhood.

I stand before the men in my beige attire, my hair tied back behind my head, barely a trace of makeup on my face to distract from how eminently fucking sensible and rational I am.

"I AM A FREE WOMAN," I declare. "And you are mad cultists!"

Cosmos tries — and fails, to hide his smirk. I'm sure any of the others here would get up and try to shush me, but in spite of being a murderous psychopath, he's not the kind of man to silence a woman. I appreciate that about him. Also, he continues to be incredibly fucking hot.

"Holy shit," I hear Anita whisper behind me.

"Cosmos," Bryn says. "It would seem your wife is feeling unwell."

"I've NEVER felt BETTER," I disagree.

"You're drunk," Bryn growls. He doesn't like this interruption. He doesn't like this attitude. He doesn't like a woman who knows her mind. He prefers a nervous young woman with all the self-determination of the average bit of wet toast.

"I am drunk," I say. "But in the morning, I will be sober, and you will still be a cult leader."

"Cosmos, take your wife to bed before I take her to my office and cane her," Bryn says.

"I'd like to see you try! Cosmos is teaching me to fight!"

"We haven't actually started any of those lessons," Cosmos reminds me.

"I watched you today," I say. "How hard can it be?"

And then, suddenly, unexpectedly, there's a sword in my hand. Fuck knows where that came from, but I can feel the silk-wrapped grip against my palm, and the shine of the blade catches the candle lights of Direview with an anachronistically threatening gleam.

Everybody is staring at me, and I do mean everybody, from Cosmos to Bryn, to the unflappable Crichton himself. I find myself the center of stunned attention, caught right in the middle of complete silence.

Thor leans over to Bryn. "That's an angelic blade."

"I know," Bryn says. "My god, I know."

I swish it about and it cuts through reality. Bits of existence peel around me. Worlds float about the place in slivers of possibility, and shards of time tinkle around my feet in a cascade.

The Brotherhood start panicking immediately. There's cursing and flailing and the sound of things they probably don't want breaking being shattered in multiple dimensions.

I can hear Bryn's desperate cry over the sound of everything being ruined.

"Get that off her before she destroys the world!"

"Easy there, little one," Cosmos purrs. He's suddenly behind me, and his hand is on my wrist, controlling me. "How about we sheath that?"

His other arm is wrapped around my waist, snugging me back against the hard lines of his body. I feel him anchoring me to the world I know, pulling me back from the brink of madness.

Just like that, the sword is gone. I don't know where it came from, and I'm not sure where it went, but four tumblers of brandy make that a concern for another day.

"Christ," Thor curses. "I have never seen anything like that in my life."

"You have a hammer that brings down the fury of the heavens," Cosmos reminds him.

"That's a real artifact. She summoned that sword out of thin air. I've never seen that done before. It's written about in some of the very ancient tomes, but the power it takes to actually do it..." Bryn is impressed.

I am sleepy. A yawn escapes me as my head rolls back onto Cosmos' shoulder. He's supporting me, holding me up. I feel suddenly exhausted. And soft. And warm. And happy. And okay. It is as though a tight string that has been held taut inside me for years is suddenly cut. I'm free.

"Well," Anita's saying. "There's her angel power. Sort of makes your weather-based one look..."

"Yes," Nina says. "It's crazy."

Does she sound jealous? I think she sounds jealous. That strikes me as funny for some reason. I start to giggle and it soon becomes almost impossible to stop.

"Alright," Cosmos says. "Bed time for you, I think."

He carries me off to bed, which as a drunk person just feels like the world is moving around me as I flail in the arms of my lover until finally, we reach a soft place.

"You're so sexy," I tell him. "I never thought I would ever be with someone sexy like you. And you married me. So you have to sleep with me forever. You have a big cock."

"And you have quite the mouth on you when you're tipsy," he says, laying me down on the bed. He starts to undress me, taking off my sensible clothes one layer at a time until I am in my panties and nothing else. I shove my thumbs into the waistband of my underwear and try to push them down in an alluring way, but somehow, I end up tangled in them.

"Sit up," he says, holding one of his t-shirts.

He slips it over my head and helps me navigate the cloth labyrinth. Then he holds a glass of water to my lips and tries to cajole me into drinking when all I want to do is kiss him.

C*osmos*

My sweet, sensible little bride is like a succubus. She's drunk, and she's horny, and she's cute as hell. I know she wants to get laid badly, but I'm enough of a gentleman to not take advantage of a sloppy drunk who could easily accidentally summon a weapon mid-sex.

"I knew you were special," I tell her as I ease her back into bed. "You should have seen the looks on Bryn and Thor's faces. You have a gift more rare than any of us have encountered before."

She makes an incoherent sound, and I am certain that in the morning she is going to find some rationalization to explain away what she did today. It doesn't matter. We have seen what she is capable of now, and her training just became that much more important. An angel blade in the hands of a person without weapons training is mass casualties waiting to happen.

For now, she's curling up into the bedding like a kitten kneading its mother's stomach. She's adorably comfortable. Watching her brings me a kind of peace I haven't felt before. Elise makes me want to keep her safe. I feel protective. I feel like a husband should.

9

E*lise*

"Ungghhh."

I wake up to birds shouting directly into my earholes with the force of a 747 taking off, or at least that's what it feels like. The moment I open my eyes, I wish I hadn't.

"Well," Cosmos says. "You made quite the scene, didn't you."

"Oh, fuck," I curse, not for any particular reason, but just because the moment seems to demand it. "My head."

"There's water by the bed," Cosmos says. "Sit up and sip it. Not too much at once. I'll get you a bucket."

I didn't drink that much. Or maybe I did. I don't know. I don't usually drink at all, so maybe a few whiskeys was enough to put me over the edge. The previous evening is fuzzy. I know I did something wrong. There's just that sort of little void in my stomach that tells me I've fucked up even though I can't remember the exact specifics.

"Bryn wants to talk to you," he adds.

"I don't really want to talk to anybody," I say. "I want to get back to the computers. I had some ideas yesterday that I never got to…"

"I don't think you're going to be spending a lot of time on the computers today," Cosmos says. "It's going to be a very educational day for you, learning about yourself and…"

"I'm not interested in educational. I need a nap."

"You're not going to get a nap. Keep that in mind next time you get the butler to ply you with spirits. We have to deal with Bryn."

"Oh. God. No," I whine. I don't want to talk to Bryn. He's the big, solemn, overly muscular and domineering dark cloud around which the rest of this household orbits. His kindness is conditional and his attitude toward me is somehow almost as possessive as Cosmos'.

"Like it or not, what you showed Bryn last night is not something he's going to forget anytime soon. Let's get it over with."

"But I'm hungover."

"I know. That's your punishment. Isn't it neat and tidy how life takes care of some of these things for itself."

"I need breakfast."

"I think in your current state, deferring breakfast is probably wise. Let's get this out of the way. Wash your face, get dressed, let's go."

～

I appear before Bryn feeling like death warmed over. I'm wearing a crisp white blouse and dark black pants, which makes me feel much more anchored to what I consider to be reality. He's summoned us to his office, a room that feels like the principal's office.

I give Cosmos a pleading *do we really have to do this* look. He gives me a little shrug. I think he's proud of the madness that occurred last night. He has a particular love for chaos that usually admire or fear, I guess, but right now I don't know what he wants from me — or what any of them want from me.

Bryn is sitting behind a big oak desk. He has a five o'clock shadow around his jaw. He looks like he had a late night. I wonder what he did after I... what did I do? Surely what I'm remembering is wrong. I have faint memories and vague impressions of pulling off an incredible magic trick, of making the world break for me. I'm starting to think that brandy wasn't just brandy. Probably had some kind of mushroom infusion. That's what probably happened. A trip. That makes sense.

"Did you sleep well, Elise?" Bryn starts the conversation with an almost fatherly question. I am not buying it. He doesn't care how I slept. His gaze is locked on me with dark intensity. There is something very dark about Bryn, far darker and more dangerous even than the demon Crichton, or anybody else I have encountered thus far. When I am near him, I feel my skin prickle the way it does around a predator.

"Sure," I say. "Thank you."

"Do you know what happened last night?"

"I got drunk and made an idiot of myself."

"You summoned an angelic weapon," Bryn says.

"I don't think that's what happened. I think the brandy was spiked and we were all drinking it and I think we imagined…"

Bryn has no patience for my rationalizations. "It was real, and it was very, very dangerous. You'll take this seriously, and you will not be allowed the luxury of denial anymore. You are an angel, girl. Accept it. You may be the most powerful angelic warrior to walk this Earth in a thousand years. Your ongoing refusal to accept even the slightest bit of reality begins to grate." Bryn is speaking through clenched teeth, his dark eyes smoldering with annoyance. I really piss this guy off. And I'm really enjoying that.

"Wow, grate? I had no idea. Let me believe in whatever garbage you need me to in order to continue your mad crusade against basically nothing."

Bryn glowers at Cosmos. "You need to get this woman under control. She lacks discipline. She treats her celestial gifts as if they are mere illusions. It's dangerous. And its offensive."

"Sure," Cosmos says, running his hand through his electric blue hair. "I'll get right on that." His tone suggests he doesn't care that I'm out of control, that he enjoys my wildness and my sass. I glance at him and we share a smile.

Bryn sits back, his palms flat out on the oak table in front of him, his black shirt open a couple of buttons, the cross around his neck never having meant less.

"If I have to, I will break the both of you," he growls. "Do not make the mistake of thinking just because this is England, I will treat you in a civilized fashion if you continue to defy me. Cosmos, we have history, but I think you know how important this is. How important Elise is."

Cosmos is as cool as Bryn is angry. I can tell that Father Bryn is used to being in control, and that he really loathes he has to defer to the black sheep of their family on this one.

"Sure," he says. "But it is her gift. It's not yours to control. I know it is hard for you to fathom there being something in this organization that isn't yours to control, but here we are."

"You're a cocky little shit, Cosmos. But you also know how to do what has to be done. I trust you'll do it. And I hope you know that if you don't, it will be done regardless."

"What will be done?" I ask the question. I want to force him to make the threat.

"You'll be made to learn the lessons you need to learn in order to become what you can be, and to stop you from being a danger to existence. That angelic blade can cut from here to Hell and back, and you have no way of controlling it."

"Don't worry," Cosmos says, dropping his arm around my shoulders. "I'm a very good teacher."

"Let's hope so," Bryn sighs.

"That man wants to beat you so badly," Cosmos laughs as we leave. "If he dared, you'd be so very sore right now."

"He doesn't dare, though, does he. Because I'm not his. And even if you wouldn't kill him for touching me, Nina would. He can't do anything about me."

"You do need to learn to control your power," Cosmos reminds me in the midst of my gloating.

"Maybe. Or maybe I just need to not drink half a decanter of spirits. It's not as if I've had a problem with spontaneously appearing magical blades before. It's probably just stress related."

"This isn't a bout of IBS," Cosmos reminds me. "It's a power that makes you a potential force for good in the world."

"Sure, yes, because fiery blades are always constructive. Who knows, if I hit the tequila, maybe I can come up with some kind of angelic nuke and create world peace." I snort, this is all so ridiculous. Even when I allow myself to believe in it, it's just silly.

"You were slicing reality like cheese and you're not interested in repeating the experiment?"

Smart man. He's speaking my language. Trying to lure me in with science talk. But it's not going to work. Except I think it might already have worked.

"I think repeating the experiment would involve more brandy and outrage."

"And I think you've had enough of both for one day. It's time to get some breakfast."

. . .

C*osmos*

"I do not want to go for a run."

We've had breakfast, and she's been sick. She's looking a little pale, but there's no time like the present to get started. Elise is sweet, and she's smart, but she's also the kind of spoiled you get with only-children who've never been in a relationship and who only have to worry about themselves. She doesn't do anything she doesn't want to do.

"You need to increase your fitness to outrun killers."

"I'm never going to be able to outrun a man, so why try?"

She's impeccably logical, this brat of a bride of mine.

"In a straight sprint, possibly not. But there are times it is advantageous to be able to move faster than a shuffle."

"But..."

"Elise. Sweetheart. I've been very patient with you, but I promise you I will spank your ass so hard you can't sit down if you don't start doing as you're told."

"You stuffed me into a trunk. Not exactly patient."

"Would have thought that'd teach a smart girl like you a lesson in obedience."

"Everybody has a weakness somewhere. I guess mine is... ow!" She gasps as my palm meets her ass. "God, fuck, OW!" The second curse comes with the second slap. She knows I'll spank her good and hard, I'm not sure why she's pushing this. Maybe the interview with Bryn made her think we are allies against his dark authority — we are, but that doesn't mean she can get away with being lazy.

"Let's go. Three times around the grounds."

Her pout is cute. Her butt in the tight-fitting running clothes is even cuter. It's going to be hard to keep myself from spanking her. I suppose I don't really need to worry about holding back. She more than deserves everything she gets.

We make it once around the grounds, barely.

She can only jog about two minutes before her face is bright red and she's gasping for breath and begging for respite. Not exactly a physical specimen, but I already knew that, and she's cute as a button anyway.

"I'm not made for this," she gasps, hands on her knees. "I'm not going to survive this. Leave me here."

E *lise*

"Outside the front door? You little drama queen," he laughs, picking me up. My husband carries me over the threshold of Direview and back toward the basement arena of weapons training. I can't believe he expects me to keep exercising. Can't he tell I'm not made for this? I belong at a desk, sitting in a chair with lumbar support, slowly destroying my eyesight.

"I'm really very done. I'm hungover. I'm..."

"I know. I know. Quit whining."

I shut up while I'm ahead. Cosmos takes me downstairs to the training arena, a room engineered to provide optimal conditions for well-muscled men to beat the hell out of each other. I'm even less up for this than I was for running.

"I know you're on the verge of being sick again," he tells me. "Today we're going to learn about your power, so next time Bryn lectures you about it, you can at least know what you're talking shit about. Crichton!"

He summons the demon, who, as usual, just comes in via the door like any human would.

"How can I help you, Master Cosmos?"

"What do we know about angelic blades, Crichton?"

"Little is known, as their presence on earth has been regarded as mythical even by those who believe. It is said that an angelic blade can only be wielded by one pure of mind and heart, someone with singular intention and right-eous fury."

"So it's like we thought. I have to be drunk, and or pissed off."

"We will practice with a wooden sword. You can learn the basics before you accidentally manifest some weapon of unimaginable power again. You know the gentlemen's smoking room is going to be a portal for potential demonic transmission for years to come."

"I did not know that."

"Oh, yes. You should really go and inspect the aftermath of your handiwork. Quite stunning."

"Yes. Alright. Let's go upstairs."

I return to the scene of my, well, scene.

"Well," I say. "Fuck."

There is an anomaly in the middle of the room. A messy, shattered place where the world simply isn't anymore. There are spinning bits of reality shining like glass, reflecting the light from the windows, and then a sprawling hole of isn'tness between them.

I stand and I stare. It is just as I remembered. It is an impossible possibility. It is the perfect paradox and I created it with my very own will. I have been refusing to fully buy into this bonkers belief system but seeing these remnants of destruction in the sober light of day is very convincing indeed.

"It's real," I say wonderingly.

"Yes," Cosmos agrees. "We have been trying to tell you that for what feels like a small eternity."

"Holy... I'm magical."

"Yes," he says.

I turn to him with a marvelous expression of wonder as I am suffused with an entire universe of possibility all at once. I am more powerful than I ever imagined I could be. There is a force inside me that animates me and allows me to do what should not be done. I am my very own real-life super-hero. And I have just come to a conclusion Cosmos needs to hear.

"Magical people don't do cardio," I inform him.

"My bride does, or she gets herself spanked long and hard," he replies, tapping the tip of my nose with his finger as if I am a cute, but disobedient puppy.

"I can tear holes in the fabric of being!"

"Yes, and Crichton here can travel between this world and Hell. Everybody is special here, Elise. That's why you belong."

"Bryn said I was the most special, though. Demons are a dime a dozen here, no offense, Crichton."

"None taken," he murmurs.

"But only Nina and I are angels, and her powers are mostly winsomely wandering around in the mist. I'm the real deal. I can summon the flaming sword that stood between humanity and the paradise of Eden."

"Wow," Cosmos says. "And here I was thinking you were a little atheist with no knowledge whatsoever of divine lore."

"I picked up vague bits here and there."

"Uriel was left to guard Eden with his flaming sword," Crichton says, filling in the gaps left by my patchy under-standing.

"So. This Uriel. Is he the one who knocked up my mother? Wait. Don't tell me. I don't care. I decided a long time ago I never want to know who my father is, and that doesn't change just because he's magical."

"Now do you see what a responsibility you bear?" Cosmos is coming over all serious.

"What's it for? As in, what am I supposed to do with it? You want me to guard the shrubs outside?"

"Like all gifts, you will choose how you use it. Your responsibility is to learn how to use it. And that, Elise, is why you are going to learn to fight."

We'll see about that.

10

Time passes. Not a lot of time. A matter of days, perhaps a week or two. I have done everything I can to stall Cosmos' plans for physical training. I've buried myself in calibrating the Gauss rates of the computers upstairs. That's not actually a thing, but it sounds enough like a thing for Cosmos to believe that I need to do it. Then my period came, which took me out of action for a full week in almost every sense. Can't learn how to slay evil when you're wrapped around a hot water bottle. But then I ran out of excuses, and he made me actually run. I hate it. Physical activity is not my thing.

I have started to settle in at Direview. I've begun to be treated like one of the girls. I really never thought I'd start to view these people as friends and confidantes, and I still don't. I haven't forgotten my old life, my independence, my work. I haven't forgotten what it is to be normal. God, I miss normal.

Cosmos has been busy in his own way. He and Bryn are at each other's throats almost constantly. They make good sparring partners for one another. That is another way I am kept out of training.

But inevitably, I eventually overplay my hand. It is a sunny afternoon and all I want to do is go sit in a dark room and look at my screens, but Cosmos has banished me from work for the rest of the day because apparently, I am wasting my entire existence looking at a screen. This does not please me, as it leaves me confronted with the dreary reality of Direview.

"This place is going to make me so fucking bored I'll put my eyes out for something to do," I announce. "I like the computers, but I don't want to live here. This is a place people go to rot. The whole place is decaying. What's being done here isn't right."

"It's only been a few weeks. Give it time. You'll settle in. You can do some more work tomorrow, won't that be nice?"

I've always been able to bury myself in my work, but now the prospect of doing that makes me feel as though I am just avoiding the truly important things in life.

"I need to get out of here. It's a place women go to be eaten alive. Nina's miserable. Anita's convinced she's a demon."

"She *is* a demon, Elise. That's the problem. It's not that Direview is twisted, it's that you keep fighting what your own eyes and senses tell you. You're already trying forgetting how that blade felt in your hand, aren't you? You're pushing it to the verges of your mind and looking for ways to deny it. You're hoping all of this might somehow be explained by carbon monoxide or something..."

"Carbon monoxide! Yes! That would make so much sense." I snap my fingers. "Direview probably has a CO problem, and that's probably why you all think you're angels and demons and whatnot. We should get a detection kit."

He gives me a dark look.

"Fine," I sigh. "It's all real. I'm a magical angel girl. And I'm bored."

He smacks my ass with the flat of a wooden sword. I don't know where the fuck that came from. I guess I wasn't paying attention. Too busy whining about the circumstances to notice the circumstances. "Let me unbore you, brat. Let's go train."

"I can't."

He raises a dark brow at me. "Why not?"

"The computers..."

"Are fine. What else have you got?"

"My period..."

"Ended days ago. I was inside you last night, brat. What else."

I can't think of anything else besides I don't want to, and I already know that Cosmos doesn't care if I want to. With a deep internal sigh, I acquiesce. How bad can it be?

The only good part of training remains watching Cosmos shirtless. The way his muscles work when he moves is pure poetry. It's like having my very own strip tease playing out right in front of me.

Sword play is not my forte. I remain much more interested in the archaic technology in the little green room upstairs. Unfortunately, I don't have keys under my fingers. Instead I have the firm hardness of the hilt of a practice sword.

"There are many traditional styles of using the sword," Cosmos says. "Arguably one of the most effective is Iaido, a Japanese art involving killing with the fewest motions possible. It is about refined movements, swiftness, and particular attention to angles."

"Show me."

That's what I say whenever I'm trying to get out of doing whatever it is he is doing. It has worked a dozen times before. Today it doesn't work at all.

"I'll demonstrate. You follow."

It's not that hard to do, I suppose, but Cosmos is a much more stern teacher than he is husband. He shows me a movement, and I attempt to half-heartedly emulate it while wishing the entire ordeal were already over.

"Bring your elbow in, and your... elbow in, Elise. Are you listening?"

I am already tired of this. I drop both elbows and scowl at him. "I don't want to learn how to do whatever this is! I'm not interested!"

"Don't you want to be able to take fiery revenge on those who came for you?"

"Not really."

"Wait. What?" He looks at me like a stunned, tattooed blue mullet.

"I just want a nice, quiet life. I don't need revenge. What I saw you do… you've exacted enough revenge for me several times over."

"Do you not understand how dangerous you could be?"

"I thought that was a bad thing?"

"No. It's not a bad thing. It's a strength. And it could be a gift to the world. When you refuse to train, you're not refusing it for yourself. You're refusing it for everybody. There are others who will be targeted, and who can be saved if we take the fight to Fleisch."

"Then take the fight to Fleisch. I'm not a marine. I'm not a fighter. I'm a scientist."

I drop the sword and storm upstairs. I just want to be cast in the friendly glow of a computer screen. I want to be separate from the world, observing it, safely away from anything that could actually happen to me.

I expect Cosmos to come after me — and he does. He grabs me by the arm and swings me around to face him in the middle of the kitchen. I can see disappointment in his eyes. I hate that, but I hate his plan for me even more.

"You could be so much more than what you are. From the moment we met, you've been denying your potential. But you can't change what you are, Elise. You denied your angel blood, and now you are denying the gift that makes you the fighter you don't want to be. When are you going to stop fighting yourself and start fighting evil?"

"I don't know. Probably never. Before I met you, I was happy being just me.

"Before you met me you were completely unaware of what you are."

"And now I know I'm a freak. God. Cosmos. I just want to go back to the computers. Why won't you let me be who I am? I'm never going to be your perfect warrior woman."

"You've never had any problem fighting me," he points out. "You disobey and defy me at every turn. Why can't you channel that contrary energy toward the enemy?"

"Because I don't care."

I sound petulant. I am petulant. Whatever. I don't care.

With the worst timing in the world, Bryn enters the kitchen. Maybe he's there for a snack. Or maybe he's come to do some more lecturing. That seems to be the purview of these dark masters of the occult.

"Ugh!" I grunt at seeing him and carry on my way. I am done with being lectured by men who think they know me better than I know myself.

C osmos

"Trouble in paradise?" Bryn asks the question with a raised brow.

"She's not interested in training to use her powers more effectively in combat. I don't understand it. She was almost killed twice, and she doesn't care."

I expect him to give me another lecture about teaching my bride a lesson. Instead, he is strangely sympathetic.

"This is all very new for her. She's a logical little thing, and I am sure that this world she's found herself in has shaken the foundations of her understanding of everything, including herself."

"It's so much wasted potential," I say. "Maybe I should take her with me into the field."

"No," he shakes his head. "That is a terrible idea."

"One way or another, that gift was not made to be hidden away. It is time we took the fight to Fleisch and recovered their relic. Once we take that away from them, they're done. No more angelic blood trade."

"Fleisch doesn't keep that relic in a sandwich bag in their office safe. We don't know where they have it, but we can guarantee it will be kept behind an endless series of doors and safes, walls within walls, and guarded by a series of ever more violent and nasty men and perhaps demons. It is impenetrable. In every way."

"Except we now have someone who can cut through reality itself. It doesn't matter what they have guarding it, or where they are hiding it. She can obliterate it. She can end this infernal war. It could be over. Fleisch could be destroyed. Forever."

Bryn likes the sound of that. He's starting to smile. He's finally seeing what I saw the moment fire extended from her palm and formed a blade. My bride has the potential to be the end of evil, or at least, one very specific form of it.

"You do know you'd be risking her life."

"I would not be. I would be with her. And you would be with me. And Thor. And perhaps even Anita, that little demon has potential all of her own. And the rest of the Brotherhood. I am talking about one final assault, one last stand, the culmination of a hundred years of destiny."

Bryn smiles. It's a rare expression on his face when he's speaking to me.

"You're right," he says. "But she needs more than two hours of training. I want to see her at peak performance before we attempt to assault the very core of Fleisch. I assume she knows this is your intention?"

"Well…"

"Cosmos. She'd be putting her life at risk. You'd be putting her life at risk."

"I'd never let any harm come to her."

"You wouldn't be able to stop it. Once a battle begins, casualties are guaranteed. And she would be the tip of the spear. You could lose her."

"Look at her power, Bryn. She's the answer to everything."

Bryn holds up a warning hand. "Take it easy, Cosmos. She has a gift, but she's not the chosen one. She might have angelic blood, but she's still very human."

"I'm just saying. At some point, we have to take the fight to Fleisch. We have to eradicate them. You think I carry around bloodied heads for fun?"

"You? Yes. Yes. I do."

"Alright. I'll give you that. But Bryn, she could change everything."

He shakes his head. "She might be ready one day, but I can promise you today is not that day. Everybody at Direview has a purpose to serve, and none of us are going to reach our destiny any quicker by trying to rush. You're right when you say a war is coming. But let it come."

"You were just telling me I needed to teach her as soon as possible..."

"I told you she needed to be gotten under control. I did not tell you that you had to turn her into an assassin in a day. You're going to have to be patient, Cosmos. I know that doesn't come naturally to you. Elise is going to challenge you in many ways. Now. You might want to go adjust that attitude of hers before it becomes entrenched."

I take Bryn's advice and go and find my wife. It's not hard to find her. She's fled to the computers and is tapping away on the keyboard when I enter the room.

"I'm not doing any more exercise," she says, refusing to pull her eyes away from the screen. "I don't care what you do to me."

I've done enough talking for one day. I'm obviously not going to argue or cajole her into doing as she's told. That suits me fine. I know how to handle a naughty little girl who doesn't want to listen.

I snag Elise out of her computer chair, take the chair myself, and pull her squirming, cursing body over my knee. She feels perfect over my lap, her weight, her curves, the tension in her muscles making her a perfect little package to be disciplined.

"You'll do as you are told, brat," I tell her, landing a hard slap to her rear. She gasps and lets out a little curse under her breath. "If I tell you that you're going to train, you're going to train. Your only choice is whether you do it comfortably, or if you do it very, very sore."

"You're a bully!"

"I am your husband and your master. I am your beginning and your end. You will obey me, Elise, either willingly and with grace, or reluctantly and in pain."

Fuck. I sound like Bryn. Gross. I always thought I'd be the cool husband, the one who let his wife be who she wanted to be and do what she wanted to do. But Elise is making that absolutely impossible.

I peel down the leggings and underwear that protect her modesty and I set about spanking her pretty rear with several dozen hard slaps delivered in a swift staccato, turning her cheeks bright red in under a minute. She's more tender than she realizes. When she opens her mouth and sasses me, she forgets that this is a possibility. I'm going to make sure she remembers.

"Fucking OW! Cosmos! Stop! Please! Fuck! Stop!" She's begging and cursing and wishing she'd behaved herself in the beginning, but it is already too late. She's going to get a proper spanking, the kind of spanking that doesn't stop until a lesson is irrevocably learned.

I paint her ass pink with my palm, listening to her plaintive squeals and wails and feeling myself harden at each and every one of them. She calls me a sadist, and that is an accurate term. Unfortunately for her, my bride is not a masochist. She doesn't like this pain — and that makes delivering it even more satisfying.

She could have obeyed. She could have done as she was told. I would have praised her and petted her and rewarded her if she had just been a good girl. But she wanted to be bad, and now she is destined to cry over my thighs, her sobs music to my ears.

"You're hurting me!" She wails the words, as if they will be some kind of revelation.

"I know," I tell her, my voice deep and rich with satisfaction. This spanking is designed to hurt, and to shame. She will not sit easily for quite some time. She will perhaps loathe me for it, but she will respect me and she will obey me next time I give her an order.

Her pretty ass is not the only target of my stern slaps. Her upper and inner thighs also make themselves available targets as she flails in the helpless attempt to avoid punishment. She brought this on herself. She knows what I am, and she knew better than to defy me. It has been too long since she was punished. I will make every part of her sore if I have to.

"Please! Please! Ow! I'm sorry! Ouch! Cosmos!"

Her begging is not making me feel in any way merciful, but it is turning me the fuck on.

"On your knees," I growl, pushing her down from my lap to the floor. A good, tamed bride belongs on her knees before her husband. Elise has not shown proper respect from the beginning. I've been too soft with her, too aware of her feelings and too encouraging of her rebellions. She doesn't know what's coming next. She thinks I've taken mercy on her. The truth is far harsher than she imagines.

My cock springs free from my pants as I loose the zipper. One of my hands is curled in the back of her hair. The other fists the base of my cock. I bring the two elements together, her hot, wet mouth, and my rigid, unyielding dick.

I fill her mouth with my cock, her tearful gaze making me throb. I am so fucking close to coming already, but I don't want to just fill her up. I want to fuck her mouth first. I want to use this hole of hers, the one she uses to sass me with and defy my will.

She makes the most adorable sounds as I do just that, thrusting all the way to the back of her mouth before pulling out and repeating the process. I am punishing her as she deserves to be punished and using her the way she should be used. She's still trying to cry, and the motion of her tongue against the underside of my cock as she gasps and whimpers around my hot rod is what sends me over the edge. I roar as I come down her throat, keeping her golden hair fisted firmly as I ensure that she takes every drop.

·   ·   ·

E *lise*

I taste cum and shame. My ass is burning and swollen, my inner thighs are stinging, and my lips and eyes are swollen with two different reactions to the same punishment. He made me cry and he didn't care. I think he liked it more when I cried. When his tattooed arm held me in place as his thick cock plunged all the way to the back of my throat, I thought I might choke on his cock. But he was just careful enough not to do real damage.

"Get up," he says, his eyes cold. "We're going to train. Or I can get the cane, and we can see how you work with a welted ass."

When I hesitate, he grabs my hair again and lifts me up from the ground that way, forcing me to use my legs to stand.

"I have been kind to you," Cosmos growls. "But, Elise, sweetheart, I enjoy being cruel to you even more. Be careful what cause you give me to punish you. Your tears are a powerful aphrodisiac."

He's sick, and he's twisted, and I can't escape him.

Cosmos marches me back downstairs, all the way into the basement where I am once more presented with the wooden sword I threw down in a fit of temper not twenty minutes ago.

I can barely see him through the glaze of tears that fills my eyes. I am not cut out for this treatment or this life. I want to collapse into a pile of self-pity, but he won't allow that. I've crossed him, gone from being an ally against Bryn to a problem he has to solve.

He wants me to work out, but there's no way that's going to happen. I'm in no state to exercise. I am sore and in spite of my promises to obey, obedience is the last thing to come naturally to me.

Cosmos is not stupid. He sees that all at once and absolutely completely. I feel as though I am an open book to him, my pages laid bare, shameful truth scrawled in a hand only he can read.

"Bend over the horse," he says, pointing to a vaulting horse. I immediately conclude he wants to punish me more.

"No! Please. I'm sorry. I'll be a good girl."

"It's too late to be a good girl."

I do as I am told, because that look in his eye tells me that things can still go from bad to worse. There's always a darker level of depravity where Cosmos is concerned.

He runs his blade down the gap between my cheeks, absolutely ruining the pants he brought me recently. The action bares my ass again, but he's not interested in whipping me. I don't feel the anticipated slashing cut of the cane as it meets my skin. Instead, I feel his big hand part my cheeks, and the thick, hot head of his cock nudge up between my thighs.

He's inside me. I'm dripping wet. His cruel treatment has turned me on more than I can say. I must be a twisted, broken little thing to enjoy this. I can hear myself moaning, and I can feel the way my hips are grinding in response to the way his cock stretches me deep.

"Fuck. Fuck. Fuck. Fuck." I punctuate every one of his thrusts with profanity. The harder and faster he thrusts, the less coherent I become, until I am emitting wails of almost continuous cursing. I am being fucked out of my mind, my thoughts evaporating into needs, and those needs taking complete control.

He's made me submit, not just to him, but to my own filthy needs, to the most basic levels of my being. When he handles me this way, I am not a human, and I am certainly no angel. I am an animal being bred by a rough and dominant male, and it is everything I need.

He leaves me awash in fresh flows of seed, filling my pussy the same way he filled my mouth, his thick cock throbbing deep inside my sensitive tissues. I lift myself up from the vaulting horse slowly, feeling the blood rush back to its proper places. I ache so beautifully and so completely, I cannot tell what is the aftermath of pleasure and what was intended to be punitive.

"That's better," Cosmos purrs, putting his cock away.

I do feel better. But I do not feel any more like becoming Direview's ultimate fighter than I did before. I'm just not interested, and in spite of his insistence and punishment and pressure, it's not going to happen.

I can still feel the ache in my ass, taste his cum in my mouth. I can feel the effects of everything he has done to me, of all his efforts to subdue me to his will. But my will remains strong.

Turning around, I look up into his eyes. "You cannot make me want to fight. You can punish me. You can lecture me. You can shame me. But you cannot change me. I will never willingly train with you. You will have to get your exercise from whipping me."

He growls like an animal. I brace myself for a fresh onslaught of dominant discipline. But it doesn't happen. Instead of grabbing me and beating and fucking me all over again, he looks at me and shakes his head.

"I'm going for a walk."

11

*C*osmos

I need to clear my head. My wife drives me to distraction with her native contrariness. I understand it. I even admire it. But I cannot tolerate it. She has to learn to use her gift. She just has to. Beating her isn't convincing her and bullying her won't work. She's the most indomitable brat I have ever encountered. Bryn can't help me, because Nina has a much softer, more compliant temperament. Thor might be of use, but he's in Norway. I am left to my own devices and to the growing realization that Elise might not be breakable. She may always be precisely who she intends to be in any given moment, and that, I think, might be what I have come to love about her most.

It's a revelation that could be truly transformative, if not for the fact that I am about to be rudely interrupted.

"Oh hello!" A broad American accent catches me off guard as I walk in Direview's gardens. I turn around to see a forty-something-year-old woman, groomed to within an inch of her life. She has platinum blonde hair beneath a wide-brimmed Carmen Sandiego hat, she's wearing dark sunglasses on an overcast day, and a pantsuit that would make Hillary Clinton immediately jealous. Her features are somewhat obscured by sun wear and makeup, but she seems to be pleasant enough, if not somewhat lost.

"Hello." She smiles brightly. "I'm Katya Montaigne. I've a great interest in genealogy, and according to my research, some of my ancestors lived in this region over three hundred years ago, would you believe it?"

Americans love it when they find somewhere their ancestors lived. That's what happens when there are wines that have been around longer than your country has existed. A yearning for historical relevance drives a lot of the tourists around these parts. Me, I'm comfortable barely knowing anything about my heritage and history. I look forward, not back. Whatever ancestors lie in my history are honored by my life, not my navel gazing.

"Is it at all possible to look inside? I know it is a private residence, but oh, it is so beautiful."

"Father Bryn usually oversees any tours, or Crichton. Let me see if I can find one of them for you," I say. I'm not in the mood to act as a tour guide. I know Elise is somewhere inside, keeping her rebellion burning at the computer. I have a feeling that today's punishment and training will not sink in easily, and that I will have to deal her further consequences soon. If she rebels, another treatment will have to follow. If she sulks, well, I suppose I will handle it in much the same way.

"Bryn!" I shout for him from the main foyer.

"He's probably in his..."

She's pulled a gun.

It's a cute little snub-nosed thing, but it will kill me the same as any other weapon would.

Bryn comes downstairs, glowering at the interruption. "Cosmos, I have a phone, or you could come up and..."

"Father Bryn," Katya says. "So nice of you to join us. Are there any other members of the little club yet to come? No? Yes? Where is the strapping Nordic hotness?"

"Thor is in Norway."

I have to give Bryn credit. He's cool under pressure. Ice fucking cold. We look at one another, giving little shrugs of resignation. Hopefully, the girls have the sense to stay away from this scene.

Katya waves the tip of her gun at the pair of us, ushering us into the front drawing room. She seems to know the layout of the place, which is not impossible as the drawings of the floor plan are freely available on a wide variety of heritage sites.

"The two of you will have to do, I suppose. I'm going to banish your service demons, just for a little bit, mkay?" She pulls a crystal vial from her pocket and murmurs an incantation or three. Who is this woman who knows the deep magic?

"Have a seat, gentlemen," she says. "Get comfortable. This is a discussion you'll want to pay attention to."

We sit, and she walks over to the door, locking it.

"There," she says. "Now we can speak uninterrupted."

She seats herself across from us and removes her sunglasses, revealing a pretty face and piercing blue eyes. She's certainly in her forties. It's not just her appearance that tells me that, it's her energy. She's poised and calm in the way only a woman with some experience in madness can be.

"I actually owe you two a debt of gratitude, or rather one of you, the blue-haired one. What's your name, sweetheart?"

"Everybody calls me Cosmos," I say.

"Of course they do. Well, Cosmos, you cut off my predecessor's head, which I have to say really helped me break through this particular glass ceiling."

She's Fleisch. The beast has grown a new head. A female one, this time.

"We've been aware of your activities for a long time, of course, as our archnemeses. We know all of you. We know your weaknesses and your strengths. We've allowed you to continue to exist as an amusing anachronism, but lately your hostility has become untenable. I, of course, refer to the beheading of my predecessor. I would be loathe to experience the same fate. So. I've decided to take action. Would you like to know what course of action I've chosen? It's a very good idea."

"Please, enlighten us," Bryn says.

"I'm going to take your two angel brides, and I'm going to keep them hostage. I promise I won't touch their blood. They'll remain your perfect, sacred vessels. But if you continue massacring my people at the slightest provocation, I can promise you they will be punished in your stead."

"We will never let you take our brides. Any attempt to do so will be met with an avalanche of violence," Bryn declares.

Katya smiles as if that does not concern her.

"Fleisch will be heading in a new direction. The old guard was only concerned with reanimating the flesh. I am not a spiritual guardian of the relic. I am a woman who sees an opportunity. Angelic blood is a panacea for a host of ills. Our laboratories are using it to develop cures for everything from menstrual cramps to earthquakes."

"That makes no sense," Bryn says.

"Perhaps not to you, an archaic, woefully outdated relic of times very much gone by. I know how to harness power, boys. I know how to ride the waves of chaos. That's why I came here, to talk to you. And to make it abundantly clear that the dynamic you've been enjoying, of attacking our laboratories and slaughtering our staff has come to an end. You'll need to find something new to entertain yourselves with."

"As long as you corrupt the blood of angels with your worldly concerns, we will oppose you."

"And that's why I've taken your brides."

"What do you mean, taken?"

"I already have them."

"That's not possible, we were both with our partners moments ago. I just left Nina upstairs."

"And my agents on the roof have already taken her. I did not come unprepared, Father Bryn. And believe me when I say I did not announce my presence until both Nina and Elise were securely in my custody."

I stand up, with the full intention of choking her until she returns our partners. Katya's eyes narrow a fraction and she gestures down with the nose of the gun.

"Sit, sweetheart," she says. "I will shoot you if I have to, and I'd be justified in doing so too, considering the little rampage you went on recently. You left our German laboratory looking like an slaughterhouse. You do have a flair for the dramatic, don't you. Almost artistic." Her eyes swivel to Bryn. "He appears to have mastered the art of calligraphy in the medium of large intestine."

Bryn palms his face and makes a muttered appeal to a very specific deity. "Jesus fucking Christ."

12

E*lise*

The world has gone very dark. I am being abducted. I know this because it is not my first abduction. Thanks to Cosmos I am very intimately familiar with how it feels to be transported against my will, though the way I'm being dragged and tossed about is rough, even for him. With a hood over my head, my hands bound behind my back, my ankles in a similar state, my major sentiment is *oh no, not again.*

"Cosmos? Are you trying to teach me a lesson?"

"Shut up."

The voice that answers has a German accent. I don't think this is Cosmos. I can hear someone else too. Another girl. Oh. I recognized that voice. Nina is making polite sounds of complaint, saying that the bindings around her ankles are too tight, and could they possibly loosen them, please?

She is greeted with the same terse, curse-based response I enjoyed.

There are clunks, the revving of an engine, and then speed happens.

We are being driven along the winding country lanes of Direview at speed. They're trying to get us as far away from our protectors as quickly as possible.

"This is a bad idea," Nina tells them. She's so polite. Too elegant to scream curses the way I feel inclined to. "You should let us go."

"Shut the fuck up."

They're really angry, which seems unfair, as we are the ones being abducted and surely, we're the ones who should be testy.

Outside, we hear thunder clap and the drum of torrential rain bursts around us, hammering the roof of the van. What a meteorological inconvenience for our captors. It is almost as if this abduction is cursed by a power greater than those who have stolen us away from our homes.

A sudden impact makes the van skid suddenly. I have no way of protecting myself from the crash. It is pure luck, or perhaps fate, that I have been wedged against the front panel, which doesn't make suddenly coming to a halt any better, but it does mean I don't smash my skull into steel from a distance. Small mercies.

What happens next happens quite fast. The adrenaline makes the fiery blade sprout from my hands, cutting through my bindings. I reach up with the hand not burning with divine vengeance and push the hood up and out of my eyes. What I see is the interior of a van that is clearly in a ditch. Our captors were not wearing their seatbelts, and their skulls were not as fortunate as mine. I stand up, swing around, and run eternal fire through the neck of the nearest abductor. It cauterizes as it burns, but that doesn't make the aftermath any less horrific. There's now a head rolling around in the van. I swing around and in the very next motion I cut through another part of another person.

"Fuck! Fuck! Argh! Fuck!"

"Elise!" Nina calls me. "Let me out. Without killing me. Please."

I'm half scared to go near her, but she needs me. It takes real effort to make the fiery blade retreat a little. I don't need a machete of divine retribution. I need more like a pocketknife of divine convenience.

I breathe and try to calm myself down, but not too much. I don't want it going out completely. Fortunately, it's pretty easy to maintain a reasonable level of stress while surrounded by dismembered and charred flesh.

Crouching down next to Nina, I grab her, and cut her bindings swiftly. I don't know how long I'll have this little dagger of divinity in my grip. The second I get her feet untied, she's gone.

"Holy shit, how did she move that fucking fast?"

There's nobody left alive to answer me. Turns out, Nina doesn't just have the ability to see things in mist. She moves like a cartoon roadrunner. Zoom zoom and she's fucking out of here. Angel speed is apparently a thing. I wonder why they didn't mention that before. Did they forget?

That leaves me behind, wishing I had paid a little more attention to what one does with a flaming sword of vengeance. To be fair, it fairly quickly turns out that you can do practically anything you want with a flaming sword of vengeance. It's very effective on everything and anything.

I stumble out of the back of the van to find that we didn't hit a tree as I expected. A small, but apparently mythic hammer is embedded in the engine block. Anita's dark little figure stands in the middle of the road. I'm not so alone after all.

"What is that? How did you..."

"Oh, that's Thor's hammer. He usually hates when the hammer follows my will, but I think on this occasion, he'll make an exception," she says. "I wish he'd been here to see this. Might be my most heroic moment yet."

It might be mine too. The pelting rain does not dim the flame of my blade even a little, but it does make the falling drops sizzle and burst out of existence, popping brightly around me in a halo of fire.

I have many questions, but at the same time, I have no questions. I can feel the power around me, the hand of what once must have been known as the divine upon us. Anita opens her hand, and the hammer comes spiraling back to her. It is not as large as I would have expected, but it is obvious what it is. We are surrounded by ancient power flowing through us. We are blessed, and we are cursed. We are angelic and we are demonic. And we are going home.

Nina has a head start, but she meets us by the gates of Direview. It has not stopped raining. I suspect Anita is keeping the stormy weather up by merit of keeping the scene dramatic. I suppose it is also keeping visibility down, not to mention providing a cooling system for the fiery dagger I now hold. The blade does not have a particular size or shape it has to be. It is what I need it to be.

"There's a lady in there with a weapon," she says. "She's talking to Bryn and Cosmos. I think she's threatening them. Telling them that she has us and if they don't let her operate freely, she'll kill us."

"I think we should go in there and make it very clear that's not going to happen," I say.

"The doors are locked."

"It's fine. We'll go in through the wall."

"I can't go in there," Anita says. "She already banished Crichton and Crocombe, and she's got a holy water barricade. I'll melt like a witch in one of those, you know, the movies."

"I, uh…" Nina adds. She looks pale and afraid, which I understand. She is not the one who finds herself a weapon of the divine. She's a pretty angel who could really shake up the Olympic sprints.

"Don't worry," I tell Nina. "I can do this on my own."

Is there a little bit of joy in slicing through several feet of ancient stone to gain ingress to our hostage husbands? Yes. There is. The blade flares at my will and it is as it was before, reality melting away from it, or perhaps recoiling in horror might be a better description. If Bryn didn't like what I did to the dining room table, he's really not going to like what I've done here.

I step into the room. I don't know what they call this room. Drawing room? Smoking room? Hostage room? The latter has a ring to it.

Just as Anita said, there's a woman in the room. She smells and looks expensive and put together, like she owns fifty-one percent of any company you might care to name. I feel immediately shoddy in my bloody sweats, but ever since I met these people I seem to almost always be underdressed and covered in the essence of someone or other.

"Put the gun down," I say to the woman who does indeed have a gun trained on Bryn and Cosmos. "Before I run you through with divine fire."

"Look at you," she says, keeping the gun trained on the men, but swiveling ice blue eyes toward me. "My predecessor was a moron," she says, barely moving. "You would have been such a waste to drain. You have so much more potential than anybody imagines."

I try not to feel too pleased. This is a hostage situation and people are dead and now is not the time to be basking in compliments from strange women.

"Put down the gun," I repeat. It's more grammatically correct that way, but it sounds wrong in my mouth.

She does as she's told, putting the weapon down and lifting her hands.

"Well," she says, turning to me. "What will you do with me now you have me?"

She's a very pretty woman. Very well put together. Very mature. She looks self-actualized. There's something about the way her eyes sparkle that concerns me. Obviously, it takes a certain level of cool psychopathy to pull off a heist of the kind she just did. She made a few mistakes, but the underlying plan was solid.

"If I were Cosmos, I'd cut you up into a thousand pieces," I tell her, letting the blade dip a little.

I should have had more practice. If I'd worked more with the wood sword, I'd have more control over the tip of this one. I accidentally touch the palm of her held-up hand with the tip of the sword. She lets out a scream, and I freak the fuck out, thinking I've cut her fucking hand off.

"Christ! I'm so sorry!"

Golden radiant light is gleaming from the hole in her hand. Shit. Fuck.

"You're a little clumsy with that still, aren't you, Elise," she says. Her tone is calm now. She recovers quickly, and for good reason, so it turns out.

"She's angelic," Bryn says to Cosmos, in case Cosmos didn't have fucking eyes and couldn't see the obvious before him.

"Why would an angel work for Fleisch?"

FOWMP!

That is the sound of a pair of gleaming white wings extending from the back of her lovely pantsuit. The intruder is an angel. More angel than any of us. She bleeds light, and she draws all eyes. Her presence is almost enough to distract from the way the floor in the middle of the room seems to be sort of… bubbling? There's a smell I wouldn't have associated with an angel too. A sort of sulfuric odor.

"Holy…"

"I am angelic. And a little more self-realized than any of your part blood brides," she says. "Through Fleisch, I have become more than a one trick pony. Understand this, you sniveling little priests. The powers you imagine you protect do not need protection. They are greater than you could imagine. They are…"

We don't get to hear what they are, because at that moment Mrs Crocombe materializes through the floor in a burning pool of lava and hits the angel lady over the head with a rolling pin.

BONK!

"Banish me from my old kitchen, would you." She scowls at the now insensate human angel collapsed in a pile of limbs and feathers on the floor. "Took me far too long to argue my way back up out of Hades. And for what!?"

Cosmos and Bryn move like one man, grabbing the woman. "Get her into the cells," Bryn says.

They bundle her up and take her downstairs. Anita has told me once or twice that there are prison cells down there. I've never seen them, but I imagine this lady is about to become very intimately familiar with them. How the mighty and angelic are fallen.

Over the next few minutes, things settle down. Nina and Anita come back indoors. Bryn scowls at the hole in his wall while simultaneously making a long-distance call to Norway, which apparently has a bad connection and requires him to explain loudly and repeatedly that they were held at gun point by the female head of Fleisch.

"Are you okay?" Cosmos grips me by the arms and looks into my eyes with a worried expression. He's right to be concerned. I don't know if I am okay. There are images in my head joining the ones he put there, but this time they're not his fault. They're mine.

"I. Uhm. Think so?" I don't want to think about it, so I change the subject. "What now? What happens to the lady?"

"Katya. She's above our pay grade," Cosmos says. "Even Bryn doesn't have the experience. We're going to have to call someone else in to handle her."

"Who handles rogue angels?"

"Don't worry about that. Worry about who handles you." He embraces me tightly, holding me like a precious thing

"You were so good," he says. "Such a good girl."

"I want to train more. I need to have more control over this. I don't want to accidentally decapitate someone. Again. There's a real mess out there in the rain. There's a smashed up van full of cut up dead people."

"Don't worry," he says. "We'll call Crichton back from Hell to deal with it."

"You summoned me, sir?"

Crichton's suit seems a little singed, but aside from that he is none the worse for wear. His expression is as mild as ever, though perhaps there is a certain tension around his brow that suggests he is not happy to have been forced into an impromptu journey to the depths of existential pain.

"There's a van full of dead people on the road out of here," I tell him. "I don't know if I killed them, or if I just... rearranged them after they were dead, but it's messy."

"Very good, young lady. All will be taken care of."

"What would we do without him," I sigh as he exits the room, straightening his collar. "He's the backbone of this place."

"In more ways than one," Cosmos agrees. He's still holding me tightly. I think he was afraid to lose me. I was afraid to lose me. Fleisch was never supposed to come here. We were supposed to be safe. But isn't that just the story of my life. Places that were meant to be safe turn out to be perilous. "Don't worry. It's going to be okay."

I don't know if that is true. In fact, I am pretty sure it is not true at all. But I pretend to believe because that's the comforting thing to pretend to believe.

Later that night, when all Direview is asleep, I tiptoe down a great deal of stairs to find the dungeon. I am curious about what happened today.

"Hello," I whisper to the angel lady with a headache. "I just came to say sorry about cutting a hole in your hand."

"Hello," she replies. "It's okay."

"I feel like you've made a huge mistake in coming here."

"A slight miscalculation," she replies.

"Right, but also, kind of a big fucking…"

"Yes, okay. I didn't plan on you being able to wield angelic fire. That's an incredible blessing."

"So I've been told. I also didn't mean to kill your men. I did, uhm, do that? But I didn't mean to. I just thought you should know that because there's been a lot of intentional killing lately, and I feel like accidental killing is, well…"

"Yes," she says.

She's very pretty, very poised. Without her wings extended, she looks like she's taken a wrong turn from the business lounge and ended up in a prison cell.

"So you came here just to try to stop the violence, is that it?"

"Fleisch and the Brotherhood have more in common than almost any other two organizations in the world. But I couldn't come here without being prepared to leverage something."

"Probably not people's wives, though? That's not a good idea."

"I didn't count on there being real affection there," she admits. She's being very open. I find her an engaging personality. Also, she has fucking wings, and whether I'd admit it or not, I think wings are fucking cool and I kind of want some of my own. My curiosity has always been my biggest strength. It might also be my biggest weakness.

"Bryn adores Nina, and Cosmos will slaughter as many as he needs to in order to keep me safe."

"Interesting. Men are rarely that dedicated, in my experience," Katya replies.

"Maybe one day you'll meet someone who loves you the way they love us."

She smirks at me with a sort of cynical expression. "I very much doubt that, my dear, but it's a sweet sentiment. And I appreciate the apology. You should probably go back to bed. I don't think being caught down here with me is in your best interest."

"I just wanted to know, the wings. Are they like the fire? Are they something you just got when you realized your true nature? Or are they something you worked on?"

"You want to know what you might yet become," she smiles. "It's almost a pity the abduction didn't work. I could have taught you a great deal. Now, unfortunately, I don't think we'll have the opportunity."

"You could teach me now?"

"Not from inside a cage, dear. And not while you are kept in a repressed state of marriage. These men that defend you also keep you small. It's a tradeoff you make when you accept protection. You must not become too strong to protect."

"I don't think Cosmos would mind if I got stronger. He's been encouraging that this whole time. I've been the one who didn't want to learn or to change. I've been sticking to what I know."

"I'd love to have an ongoing discussion about self-actualization," Katya says. "But these bars are hardly conducive. If I were free..."

"Would you run away? Would you bring back a small army to crush us?"

"I think I'd snap you up like the sweet little thing you are and take you home," she smiles.

I blush. It has been a long time since I met anybody who embodied what I want to be as a grown up. Yes, I'm an adult, but I'm not adult like her. In her presence I feel sort of stuck, and I don't like it.

"Cosmos wouldn't like that."

"He's the blue-haired reckless one, isn't he," she says. "He's very cute too. I guess we will see what happens. I am sure Bryn's desperate need to banish and control me will resolve in some way soon. In the meantime, you should keep your distance, little angel. I would not like to see you hurt."

It's good advice, and as I hear movement around the door and steps down to the basement, I also decide this is a good time to slip away.

"**W**here have you been?" Cosmos reaches out and snags me into bed, cuddling me up against his tattooed muscles. He's warm and I am immediately cozy.

"I went down to talk to Katya." I could lie to him, but I don't want to.

"Oh? Why?"

"I was curious. She's... she's incredible. Did you see her wings? Just being in her presence is..."

"Aw," Cosmos smiles. "You've got a girl crush."

"Don't you think she's kind of amazing?"

"Sure. She's dangerous as hell. Bryn doesn't know what to do with her. We're supposed to protect angels. None of us knows what to do with one who doesn't want or need our protection, let alone leads our enemies."

"So cool," I whisper under my breath as my eyelids start to get heavy. I am exhausted, but my imagination is alight. Katya is the first person in this place to inspire me. "Can we start training again tomorrow?"

"Yes," Cosmos chuckles. "Yes, we can."

13

E*lise*

It is a pleasant evening at Direview. It has been twenty-one days since I cut a hole in the wall, a hole that has since been boarded over. Thor has returned from the icy climes of his homeland, and we are enjoying a post-evening meal all together, the eight of us sitting around a big, round table playing cards. Crichton and Crocombe have joined us, and a gramophone plays olde timey music almost loud enough to block out the sounds of the furious angel in the basement demanding to be released.

I am perched on Cosmos's lap. He keeps cheating and looking at my cards, but he's not that great a player, so it doesn't actually matter. He's about as good at cards as I am at swordplay. I'm trying to learn, and he says I am getting better, though whether that is true or not is up for debate.

A knock at the door makes Crichton rise from his chair and head for the door. We all put our cards down and listen.

Everybody at Direview has become a little more concerned about guests of late.

"Fathers, we have a guest," Crichton announces as he returns with the knocker in tow.

The man who walks in behind him is a big, broad, bearded monster. He has to be at least six and a half feet tall. Spurs jingle on his boots, kicking up dust that isn't there.

"I heard you had a little problem with a rogue angel?"

He's got a Texas drawl and a ten-gallon hat. He's dressed fully in black, with a red neckerchief around his neck as the only splash of color. His hair is long and dark and his eyes are pale blue. I expect to see pistols at his hips, but he appears to be without weaponry, unless you count cheek-bones you could cut yourself on. He's very good looking. Very movie hero handsome. He also could not be more out of place if he tried.

I am confused.

"You sent for a cowboy?"

"They sent for a sheriff, little lady," he drawls with a wink.

"Thank you for coming," Bryn is saying, getting up and extending a hand to the ultra-American. Cosmos and I are exchanging confused looks. Apparently, Bryn's plan for Katya has not been arranged democratically. Why am I not surprised.

"Everybody, this is Sheriff Keith Starlight."

"Sounds like a 1980's cartoon," I whisper to Cosmos. He smirks. Anita grins too. She has good hearing. Thor looks generally concerned, and Crocombe and Crichton have taken their leave, sort of melting in the way good servants and demons do when they sense their presence is a problem.

"Keith has proven experience in angel wrangling," Bryn explains. "He runs a private facility in Texas where some incredible research is being done on manifestations of the divine."

"Sounds like you have a real wild one down there. I'd like to get started with her, if it's all the same to you, Father Bryn. I reckon we get her transported out of your fine establishment here as soon as possible and back to a containment unit."

"A containment unit?" I ask.

"Sure. See, an angel's inevitably going to break out of human, even demonic-built vessels. Just a matter of time. But we've got some enclosures that won't allow any angel out until Armageddon comes."

"So you build jails. For angels. Angel jails."

"That's right."

"That's terrible. Why would you do that?"

"Well, I'd say the rogue angel you have down in the basement answers that question pretty well, wouldn't you?"

"Not really. She's not that dangerous. She just wanted to negotiate with Bryn, and that's practically impossible to do without a gun."

I don't know why I am defending her. There's something in my gut telling me this isn't right. It doesn't even make sense. We're basically holding the head of a major international corporation hostage, and yes, sure, she also held Bryn up at gunpoint, but she was defeated by Crocombe's rolling pin, so how dangerous can she really be?

"Wasn't the whole point of her visit here that she wanted to do business without having her people killed? Wasn't she trying to avoid bloodshed?"

"She was trying to abduct you," Bryn reminds me. "And Nina."

"Sure. But that was more a means to an end thing. Her predecessors just sent men with knives to carve me up. In comparison..." I make that open palmed waving back and forth motion you do when you're trying to say six to one, half a dozen to the other without actually saying it.

"Well, I reckon you lot can discuss this for as long as it pleases you, but I have a flight for Texas leaving just as soon as I can board a plane. So, if you don't mind, we'll sedate the angel and..."

"How do you sedate an angel?"

Sheriff Starlight gives me a look as if my questions are starting to wear thin.

"Well, it's a proprietary blend of what I guess you might call highly concentrated holy water, and..."

"I don't like this," I interrupt him.

"Cosmos, now might be a good time to take your wife upstairs," Bryn suggests firmly, in that jaw-clenched, tight-lipped way he has when he really wants to beat someone who isn't his wife.

"Come on," Cosmos says. His arm was already around my waist. All he has to do to pick me up is snug it a little tighter and stand up. I am carried out of the room like a petulant child trying to meddle in affairs bigger than she can understand.

"He's an asshole," I growl in Cosmos' ear as he takes me out, quiet, but not so quiet that everybody can't hear me.

"Cosmos. I think we should help Katya escape and run away with her." As soon as we're out of earshot, I tell him the plan that's been percolating in my mind since I talked with her down in the cells.

He looks at me like I just told him the world was flat.

"She knows so much more about becoming angelic than anybody here. Nina knows nothing. Bryn only cares about keeping everybody in line. And I don't like this Starlight guy."

He opens his mouth, but I keep talking because I don't want to hear the *no* that I know is coming.

"You hate it here. You bicker with Bryn constantly. He treats you like a second-class citizen. There's only room for one couple here at Direview, and that's Bryn and Nina. Everyone else is like furniture for him to arrange."

"I don't get on with Bryn but betraying the Brotherhood for Fleisch is not something I'm going to do," Cosmos says. "I know you feel sorry for Katya, but this is the way it has to be."

Says fucking who.

I'd argue with him more, but the sound of a woman screaming in agony interrupts us. I race toward the sound, which is coming from the basement, where the sheriff has been given free rein with Katya.

They try to stop me, but I am smaller, more nimble, and everybody is very well aware that I can turn into a fiery ball of rage at any moment. When I arrive at the cells, Katya is shrieking. The door of her cell is open and she is caught in what I can only describe as being a forcefield of pain. Starlight's weapon is like a taser that doesn't stop tasing.

"On your knees!" he's shouting.

Katya's refusing. She's on her feet, even though she's being cramped with pain, nearly bent double. Her brilliant blue eyes are seething with angelic fury as she resists him with everything she has. I am horrified at what I am seeing. If this is what he'll do to her here, in the very heart of the Brotherhood, what will he do to her if he takes her away? My heart goes out to her, and my hand reaches for one of the wood training swords. I am putting a fucking end to this.

"Asshole!" I sweep the wood sword across the back of his knees. He goes down like the sack of shit he is. Stepping over his big body, fire leaps from my hand in a deadly blade, hovering just shy of his throat. He looks up at me in shock, as if he never thought anybody would actually stop him from hurting the woman in his custody.

"You want to use your angelic suppression device on me too?" I ask him the question fiercely. "Or do you only pick on caged women? Fucking coward."

I've never understood the impulse to spit on someone before, but I have it now. I refrain, because I am still a lady, but I think about it real fucking hard.

Katya puts her hand on my shoulder. "It's okay, Elise," she says. "I'm not hurt. Don't worry."

But I do worry. I worry because we are the ones with the power, and these men keep trying to tame us and break us and make us what they think we should be. Because they keep silencing us, and carrying us out of rooms, and putting us in trunks, and because they never, ever, fucking listen.

"I'm going to work at Katya's laboratory," I tell everybody assembled. By this time, pretty much everyone has come down. Cosmos, Nina, Bryn, Thor, Anita. Everybody's staring at me. Katya is still behind me, so I don't know how she took that piece of information.

"If she'll have me. Lab work is what I do, and none of you know what to do with a woman besides keep her on a woman-shaped shelf. Don't try and stop me, or I swear to fucking God, I will be the enemy of your worst fucking nightmares."

Bryn looks at Cosmos. "This is what happens when you don't break your bride properly."

"You're the fucking worst," I curse at him. "Break your bride? Nina should be in fucking college. So should Anita. I'm sorry for them. I'm sorry they don't have any opportunities to be anything other than your little pets and playthings. But I know the world has more to offer me. And I'm going to take it. I'm sorry, Cosmos. I know your loyalties lie here. You literally just told me that. But mine don't. And there is nothing here for me."

Cosmos has his arms folded over his chest and is looking at me with an inscrutable expression. I will miss him. I've fallen for him. But I'm not going to stay here in a world where keeping women captive and handing off the best of us to be tortured is acceptable.

I wait for him to say something, to become my ally, or take a stance as my enemy. My heart is breaking with every second it takes to get a response.

"Fuck it," he says, finally. "I'll go with you."

"You're defecting to Fleisch?" Bryn sounds shocked. Of course he is. Bryn's plan was just to get rid of the trouble-some angel woman and carry on brooding around the place.

"I'm choosing my wife," Cosmos says. "I'd go to the gates of Hell for her. I can go to Fleisch. Besides. This might be a real chance for peace. We might finally be able to stop fighting each other. People might finally stop dying. And Elise is right, Starlight is a piece of shit."

"Hey, now," Starlight says. "I'm just here to do a job."

"We're not jobs. We're not things. We're not stuff." I jab the flaming sword toward his neck, just barely missing it each time. He's really lucky I've learned more fine muscle control with this thing.

"You don't even know this woman," Bryn points out.

"I didn't know Cosmos either when I married him. Turns out knowing people before I make decisions about them is not a luxury I get anymore," I reply.

"Let the Sheriff up," Bryn relents. "And you can do as you please. Heaven knows Direview isn't big enough to contain your brand of rebellion."

"Cosmos, can you get his torture gun thing?"

Cosmos grabs that for me, and then I let the Sheriff up.

"You, little lady, deserve a good long spanking," he says, dusting himself off. He doesn't seem to bear me any ill will, but after seeing what he was doing to Katya, I don't give a toss what he thinks. Not every hot guy in a big hat matters.

"You're right," Cosmos agrees. "She does. But not for this. This is the right thing. I'm proud of her for knowing what that is. Seems like the rest of us keep forgetting."

"Letting the head of Fleisch walk is not the right thing," Bryn growls. "And working for that cursed company is not the right thing. And letting your wife lead you around by the nose is not the right thing."

"Alright," Thor says. "Enough. We're all doing what we think is best. The Brotherhood is not about following orders. It's about protecting divine blood. Or in my case, a little demon. I think this is a step in the right direction, even if it feels wrong, or rushed, or chaotic."

"I do want to go to college," Nina says. "I want to study marine biology."

"Oh for..." Bryn gives me a *look what you've done now* look.

"Me too," Anita says.

"You're not going to college," Thor says. "You'll put my bloody hammer through a lecturer's face."

"Actually, yes, I probably would," Anita grins. "But I support Nina going."

"This isn't the time to talk about this," Bryn says.

"Yes. It is. I bet she's tried to say that a hundred times before but you change the subject, or seduce her, anything to shut her up," I say. The sword is still burning brightly in my hand. I want this fixed. I want all these injustices resolved. I want to know that before I leave here I made some kind of difference.

"You better let her go to college, or I swear to almighty, I will come back with this sword and I will take Direview apart brick by brick."

"*A really good, long spanking,*" Starlight repeats, rubbing his hands together. I can only imagine what these men would do to me if I didn't have the ability to transform into a living weapon, and if Cosmos wouldn't gut them if they so much as put a pinky on me.

"Let's go," Cosmos says. "Katya, Elise, you're with me. Starlight, I hope someone turns that weapon on you one day. You come near us again and I promise I will teach you new and deeper definitions of pain."

We leave Direview as exiles. There's a heavy pall hanging over us with every step we take, and a sense of menace that I wouldn't normally ascribe to a building, but I can't help that right now. The building looms over us, the day darkening, mist rolling in behind us. England is not so much bidding us farewell as glowering at us with every ray of light and blade of grass. I hope that the others find their freedom. I know I've found mine.

14

 *few hours later…*

On a private plane over England, I toast with Katya to mutual freedom with a mimosa.

"I'm not the good guy," Katya tells me clearly. "Fleisch has a long and horrific history, and that will not be erased overnight. But I will teach you what I know, and I am sure you will do good work."

I haven't given her all my loyalty. If she does anything to cross me, she'll pay the same way anyone else would. But I'm giving her a chance, and in doing so, I'm giving us all a chance.

Cosmos has his legs extended to the seat in front of him, his eyes are closed and there's a smile on his face. He's perfectly comfortable here with me as my husband, my bodyguard, and my lover.

"Hey," I say, extending a toe to nudge him. "Do you want a drink?"

"No," he says. "Someone should stay sober to fly this thing."

"We have a pilot."

"Sure, but what if the pilot stops piloting," Cosmos winks. "I'll stay alert. You have fun, Elise. You've earned it. You turned Direview upside down. Nothing there will ever be the same. And I'm sure you'll do the same where we are going. Hope you're ready for that, Katya."

Katya smiles at me and raises her glass. "I'm counting on it."

I feel a sense of completion as we descend back toward Heidelberg. It feels like coming home, not just to a place I live, but to a place my brain lives. I'm returning to sanity, desperately needed sanity. As we land, get into a car, and are transported through the city, I start to breathe more freely. It's okay. It's all going to be okay.

The Fleisch lab is located at the edge of the industrial district. There are tall chain link fences, more than one row of them, topped with razor wire and punctuated with guard towers. I see Cosmos' dark eyes flicking across them with mild interest.

"We rebuilt the facility your husband raided," Katya tells me with a glance at Cosmos, who does absolutely nothing to acknowledge what she said. "It's much more secure now."

"Great," I say. "Sounds brilliant."

I can't wait to get into a proper laboratory. I have to admit that my curiosity is now thoroughly engaged. I'm not a geneticist by trade, but data is data, and I'm going to be at the forefront of research that potentially blends the line between science and religion forever.

"There's housing on campus," she says. "You'll have your own apartment in one of the newly built constructions, two thousand square feet of modern luxury."

Cosmos doesn't seem to care about any of this. Every time I glance over at him, he's just smiling to himself sort of distantly. It's actually creepy, or would be, if I didn't know him better.

We pull up outside the apartment building. It's not of interest to me. It's built in a vague square shape and has windows. Maybe I'll care later. For now, I want to see what I'm going to be doing.

"I'd like to go see the lab," I tell him. "Do you want to check the apartment out?"

"Sure," he says with an easygoing shrug. He's being a little weird, but I don't have time to give too much thought to that. I have craved work like nothing else.

"I'll take her to the lab," Katya says. "You settle in, and I'll have her home before you know it."

"Alright," Cosmos says, getting out of the car. "Be good, Elise."

"I always am."

"No," he laughs. "You're not."

"Don't mind him," I tell Katya as we drive away from the apartments and toward the main laboratory. "The Brotherhood has some really old-fashioned ideas about marriage."

"Men will always seek to control the blood," she says. "You see, Elise, men have always known there was a need to dominate women. Whether they like it or not, we are the portals of life itself. We are the gatekeepers and the manifesters of existence. Every woman is powerful beyond any man's wildest dreams. Those of us with the blood are even more powerful, and that drives men to dominate us even more harshly. Never forget. When someone is trying to control you, it is because they know how valuable you are."

"Cosmos would say he was just trying to protect me."

"Yes, he would say that," she smiles. "And he no doubt is, because it is not enough merely to control the blood, it must also be defended from others. He's protecting you from even worse dominators."

"Like Starlight," I suggest.

"Like Starlight," she agrees, with a small shudder. "Falling into his hands is a fate I would wish on nobody, not even my worst enemy."

"We're safe from him here," I point out as we exit the car and pass security, which I note is well-manned and tight. "Very safe, I'd say."

She smiles at me with a certain amount of indulgence and nods in what might be agreement. She's leading me through the facility now. It is big. There are a lot of halls and a lot of doors, and I'm sure I'm going to need a map to learn to get around. I'm very excited to learn what she has in mind for me.

"I've got something very special planned for you, Elise," she says, leading me down another flight of pristine white stairs.

A couple of what might be my colleagues pass us coming the other way.

"Guten Abend."

"Guten Abend," she replies.

"Guten Abend," I also say. It feels so damn good to be polite in German again. It's like coming home.

Finally, we come to our destination.

"This is the laboratory you'll be resident in."

By resident, she must mean it'll be where I work. A funny twist of phrase, but okay. I look around the room she's led me to. It's deep in the complex. In fact, if I'm not completely mistaken by the number of floors we've come down, it's about four stories underground. There's a heaviness to the area; it sort of feels draining for reasons I can't explain. The windows are very thick and reinforced. The walls must be thick too, *nobody can hear you scream* thick.

There's a bunch of monitoring equipment set up on one side of the reinforced glass partition. Banks of computers, trays of vials ready for taking samples, all sorts. I can't really see because we're on the other side, a side that has very little in the way of diagnostic equipment. It does, however, have a bed with straps attached to it, an ominous sight at the best of times. This suddenly doesn't feel like the best of times anymore.

"Katya, what..."

I hear a beep and then a clunk. It sounds like a door locking firmly behind me. I turn to look at Katya. She's smiling at me, but the smile is no longer reassuring or inspiring. It's dark and triumphant.

"Don't worry, Elise," she says. "I'm going to take very good care of you here."

"I'm not here to be a scientist," I say.

"You're here to advance science in ways it has never been advanced before," she replies. "You wield the power that sealed the garden. I cannot tell you what great significance that could have in everything from construction to weapons development."

"You want me to stay in this cell."

"You need to be kept pure," she explains. "Any contamination from the outside world will affect our readings, so yes, you'll stay here for the first phase of our studies, which really shouldn't take more than twenty-four months or so."

She wants to lock me in this subterranean box for two years. The way she's talking it almost seems as though she thinks she can actually convince me this is a good idea.

Fuck this. I will not be trapped. I extend my hand, expecting to be holding a big fuck off burning sword - but nothing happens. Not even a little lick of flame. I'm suddenly rendered normal.

Katya laughs at me. "Your power won't work here. These rooms are shielded. All angelic energy is absorbed. That means no fiery swords, and it also means no escape."

"No... what?"

"No escape, angel.

"Uhhh..." The sound that emerges from me is like a slow gurgle of realization and distress leading to one inevitable, unenviable conclusion:

Katya has betrayed me.

I'm more annoyed at myself than angry at her. What was I thinking? She presented me with the familiar and I gave into her immediately. All she had to do was present a veneer of rationality, and all mine went out the window. The Brotherhood rubbed me the wrong way, but they only ever wanted to keep me out of danger. Now Cosmos is gone, probably dead. I wouldn't let him live if I were them. His body count of Fleisch operatives is in the triple digits, last I heard.

"Cosmos isn't..."

"I've taken care of your husband."

"What does that mean?"

She's smiling at me in a very dark way. "It means nobody else has to die. And it means you're free of a marriage you likely never consented to. You can thank me now, if you like..."

I can't summon a sword of burning flame, but I can ball my hand up into a fist, rotate my hips, and strike with a straight arm with a view to smashing the cartilage in Katya's nose.

She wasn't expecting that. I feel her face sort of crumple beneath my knuckles, hard and soft and gross and wet and hot, her nostrils spurting with sudden sanguine flows. She's a much more powerful angel than I am, but in a shielded room, we are each only as good as our punches, and thanks to Cosmos, my punches are pretty fucking sweet.

I run for the door, but not before snapping her electronic pass card off her neck lanyard. Katya is stumbling around, putting her hands to her nose, then immediately wishing she hadn't, cursing to herself as I run out the door. I can't believe I actually punched someone that hard. I think I'm starting to become Cosmos. Where the fuck is Cosmos? Is he back at the apartment? I doubt it. I doubt that even is an apartment building. This whole thing has been a plan to lure me back and leech my essence.

Why did I not see this coming? Why didn't anybody else see this coming? Why did they let me do this? I'm a fucking idiot. I have to be the stupidest person that ever dumbed. If I get out of this alive, I'm never going to make another decision again.

The halls of this place are like a labyrinth. I can't remember the way I came in. Right, left, they're all the same thing.

Sirens are wailing all around me, white walls flashing intermittently red as the entire facility goes on lockdown alert to reclaim me.

I hear explosions. Loud explosions, of the kind that indicate Katya's single cross has been turned into a double cross. That's what I'm hoping, anyway. If nobody is here to help me, it's only a matter of time before the guards catch me, and I didn't spend nearly enough time training to fight all of them.

I turn a corner and run straight into the big dark form of a man. As I do, the sirens stop. The lighting returns to normal. Peace asserts itself aggressively, but wrongly.

"Hey there, little lady."

It's Sheriff Starlight. Not exactly who I wanted to see, but better than an outright enemy. In the bright fluorescent light of the Fleisch laboratory he looks even more outlandish. He's still wearing fucking spurs, as well as a waistcoat and oilskin overcoat. I should have left Katya to his not so tender mercies.

"They lied. She lied," I tell him. "This was a trap."

"We know. We've been right behind you since you left. Don't worry. It's all under control."

"Where's Cosmos?"

"He's busy doing what he does. I'm here to get you out. Let's go. This way."

I almost follow him, but then I remember my previous conclusions about not making decisions or trusting anyone. Starlight is not exactly a known quantity. He showed up at the same time as Katya did, more or less. Maybe he's on her side. Maybe this double cross is actually a triple cross.

"I'll wait for Cosmos," I say, stalling.

"There's no time. Come with me."

"No. Thank you."

Starlight grabs me by the arm and tries to pull me along. I sink my teeth into his hand hard enough to taste blood. He retaliates by scruffing me like a wild cat.

"Little lady, your husband isn't here, and I've been itching to do this since I laid eyes on your impudent angelic ass. Thing about your kind is a tendency to arrogance. Comes from the blood. You never really get away from it."

He's bending me over his leg as he speaks, and a second later, his big Texas hand is beating a tattoo on my ass. I scream at the top of my lungs. He has no right to do this to me. The shielding is still in place, and that means I can't cut him the fuck up with my burning sword of fire, but the second we're out of here, I'm going to fillet him. I swear it on my husband. Where the fuck is my husband?

"You can yowl all you like," he tells me, every slap landing firmly across my ass, making me ache. It's very different from being spanked by Cosmos. It's not hot. It's just painful. It's just some big asshole deciding he has the right to teach me a lesson because I'm not leaping to obey him.

"You're a piece of shit," I tell him. "And when my husband gets here, he's going to cut you into a thousand pieces before he lets you die. You're going to regret this, Starlight!"

"You know what all this mouthiness tells me?" Starlight speaks casually. "Tells me I'm not tanning your hide hard enough."

With that, he starts spanking me even harder. True to his word, I can't form sentences anymore. I can only screech and curse and kick and fight, none of which do anything because he has me held firmly, using his thigh to keep my hips out and my butt in his firing line.

"You'd do well with a stint at my facility," he says. "We know how to handle mouthy little angels who disobey their handlers. You'd have your bottom spanked twice a day, I reckon, probably more given the way you act. And you'd be taught proper respect, the kind that puts you on your knees before your handler and teaches you to serve. Your husband has spoiled you, let you be a headstrong little minx..."

I never find out what else Starlight thinks about Cosmos, because at that very moment Cosmos comes arcing through the air like a lithe and furious panther, the hilt of his sword held in two hands. The sound it makes as it contacts Starlight's skull is one of the most supremely satisfying sounds I've ever heard.

"Cosmos!" I scream his name and grab for him, which gives Starlight an unearned reprieve. I don't care. I want to hug my husband. I want to feel that he's okay. He is okay. As always. He's bloodied, though I don't think it is his blood that's now coming off on me. Why can't we take a trip anywhere without ending up covered in sanguine essence?

Cosmos wraps one arm around me. "It's alright," he says. "I've got you."

The tip of his blade is pointed at Starlight, who has gained his feet, but looks unsteady. That's going to be one hell of a concussion.

"You think you have the right to put hands on my wife?" Cosmos gently disentangles me, puts me behind him and advances on Starlight.

"Gotta tell you buddy, I assumed you were dead. The fighting was fierce. Couldn't get you out, so I came for her."

"Right," Cosmos says, stalking toward him. I am about to watch this guy get his fucking ass handed to him and I can't wait. My ass is aching, my pride is bruised, and I want to see some carnage.

"Cosmos!" Thor and Bryn come around the corner at speed. They're also covered in blood, also presumably not their own. "We found it!"

"Sir!" Another voice bellows. "We found it!"

There's a team of Americans coming up behind Thor and Bryn. They're dressed in black tactical clothing, holding large guns, and they're not killing us on sight, which suggests they're on our side.

"We've cleared the facility, Sheriff," the leader of their team says, with accompanying hand signals that mean nothing to me but must mean something to Starlight. "The bird is in the hand."

"Great," Cosmos says. "I just need to kill Starlight for touching my wife, and then we can go."

Starlight laughs. The fucking nerve. His hands are at his sides, fingers flexing at his holsters. "Boy, you wouldn't get another inch toward me before I dropped you. Don't be stupid. Your wife's a brat who wouldn't follow instructions."

"I know that. But she's *my* wife who won't follow instructions. Not yours."

"COSMOS!" Bryn thunders his name. "We have the flesh."

That changes the subject completely.

15

Deep underground in a hidden corner of a secret factory of twisted secrets, the Brotherhood and I uncover the final secret. Right now, Bryn is grandstanding in front of a small but sturdy silver vault located in the middle of an even bigger vault which has been accessed by explosives. They can't risk breaking into this with force, though, because this is the vessel of something so sacred all of us are speaking in hushed whispers automatically, like it's a baby we're afraid of waking up.

"This is what it's all about. This is what we and our kind and Fleisch and their kind have been dying about for more than two thousand years," Bryn whispers. "That lock can only be opened by angel blood. Elise, would you do us the honor?"

There's a finger prick device built into the front of the otherwise smooth enclosure. It's a moment of mild discomfort in return for the revelation of several lifetimes.

The machine thinks about my blood for a moment with a low hum. Then there's a hushed moment of awe as the vault swings open. And we all stare at what is alleged to be the actual flesh of a god made man.

Everybody is silent. They must be absolutely mesmerized by what they're seeing, the culmination of generations of sacrifice leading to this moment, this artifact of such deep significance the world at large can never know it exists.

I can't help it. I break the silence

"It looks like beef jerky."

"Mhm," Cosmos agrees. "It does."

"Shouldn't it, I don't know, glow or something?" Even Thor is skeptical.

It doesn't glow. It just sits there, mocking us with its mundanity. It could actually be beef jerky. It could be a decoy. How would we know? It's not as if there's a test we can run to see if it is of divine origin. I suppose we could test it to see if it is human, at least.

"We should destroy it," Cosmos says.

"Destroy a divine relic?" Bryn looks at him aghast.

"Sure. Why not. The divine won't mind. He's got plenty more where that came from. All this can do is be used for evil. We can end it all right now by destroying it."

"How do we do that?" Thor asks. "If it is truly divine, destroying it could be almost impossible."

"Could eat it. We could cut it up and we could all eat a piece of it. Like communion, but the real thing."

"That feels like a bad idea." Thor frowns.

"Maybe one of us takes a little nibble, and..." Cosmos' theorizing is interrupted.

"I'll be taking that," Starlight says, sweeping in and picking the relic up in his gloved hand before slipping it into a plastic carrier bag, where it looks more like a hiking snack than ever. "We'll keep it nice and safe in Texas, boys. No need to eat the body of the savior. I'm also taking Katya. I assume there's no objection to that. You don't really have the facilities for handling a creature like her."

There is, surprisingly, no objection to that. It might be because they don't care, or it might be because the soldiers with guns are sort of casually pointing them at the Brotherhood and we're all very outnumbered by Starlight's soldiers. The Brotherhood uses blades and hammers, and they're demon slayers, not a human assault team. Starlight has obviously lent them firepower to bring down Fleisch, an enemy of my enemy is my friend sort of situation. But now that the enemy of the enemy is gone, the friendship seems to be gone too.

"Why did you let him take the flesh?" Cosmos questions Bryn once Starlight is gone along with the relic. We have also all exited the compound and regrouped at a hotel. The television news is running a story about an unexplained industrial fire in Heidelberg. It's our fault. So many things are our fault.

"Well. For one, you were talking about eating it. For two, we don't have the infrastructure to protect it. For three, Fleisch is going to try to reclaim that, with great violence, if necessary. I'd rather they assaulted Texas than Direview. And four, I don't know if you noticed, but they stole it from us at gunpoint."

"So we lost," Cosmos frowns.

"I don't think so. We kept Elise safe, and that's all that matters."

I'm surprised. "You all came for me?"

"Yes, Elise," Bryn sighs. "We do take our responsibility to our angels seriously. You are one of us, no matter how much of a spoiled brat you are."

"So you let me go, so you could get me back, and infiltrate this compound, and get Katya and the relic into Starlight's hands."

"We let you go because some people only learn from their mistakes. You do know this was a mistake, I assume. You can never ally with Fleisch. They are our enemies. They will always be our enemies. You belong with Cosmos and with us. The world outside the Brotherhood doesn't belong to you anymore."

He might be right. I don't want to admit it, but everything they've ever told me might be right.

"When we get back to Direview, we'll see what we can do about upgrading that old computer suite," Bryn says with the air of a kindly British benefactor. "This shows me we need better security and more surveillance in general."

He's not wrong, but the prospect of returning to Direview right now fills me with a deep sense of dread. Fortunately, Cosmos has other plans.

"I'm taking Elise on vacation," Cosmos announces. "Thank you, everyone, for everything. We owe you. Big time. But I want a proper honeymoon with my wife. And I think it's time she got to enjoy something that's not part of a plot to reclaim a tasty, long-lost artifact."

"You have got to stop talking about eating it," Bryn growls.

"Why? It's part of the whole thing," Cosmos reminds him. "The lore is full of eating Christ."

Bryn sighs, clearly exhausted from fighting and from talking to Cosmos. "I'm going home to my wife. Thor, you coming?"

"Yes," Thor says. "Absolutely. Crichton and Crocombe will have had their hands full with Anita. Let's go see if Direview's still standing."

"Thank you," I say as they gather their stuff. "For coming for me. For not just... I don't know, that big speech I made, it must have been tempting to leave me to my fate."

Bryn smirks. It's not often I see wry amusement on his face. He's usually too busy glowering or glaring or growling.

"There's nothing cuter than watching someone be self-righteously wrong, only to find out what a mess they've gotten themselves in," he says. "You seem like such a logical, strait-laced little thing, and yet you littered the countryside with singed bodies, put a hole in the wall of a heritage listed building that happens to be my ancestral home, forced us to make an all-out assault in a foreign country, and you've led to the divine flesh being liberated to America, of all places. You are the most chaotic person ever to come to Direview, Cosmos included. The two of you belong together. Enjoy your honeymoon."

Two *weeks later…*

Cosmos

I'm lying on a beach on the French Riviera with my wife by my side. Elise is in an adorable little bunny-themed bikini and I'm wearing what the Australians call budgie smugglers. Sun beats down on us both in a warm embrace and the world feels good and hot and right.

But I know something's not quite right with Elise. She's been quiet, and not in a I-fell-asleep-in-the-sun way. In an adorably brooding and yet again overthinking sort of way.

"Hey," I nudge her. "What are you thinking about?"

"I feel bad for Katya."

"You shouldn't."

"I know, but Starlight was so cruel to her. And I think he enjoyed hurting her. Imagine what he's doing to her now."

"She might be someone who needs to be hurt," I remind her. "Sometimes sadism is the answer."

"Starlight deserves to be hurt," she grumbles.

Cosmos laughs. "You're still angry about him smacking your butt."

"Aren't you?"

"He was probably right. You probably did deserve it. Wouldn't hurt you to know that there's more than one person capable of keeping you in line if anything ever happens to me."

"You nearly caved his skull in for that. And I'd never let anybody else touch me. That place was shielded and I couldn't do anything about it."

"He deserved to be hit. And so did you. It was one big chain of deserved whippings."

"You make no sense," she laughs at me. "You wanted to kill him for doing it, but you also think I deserved it?"

"I'm a demon hunter in a religious cult that is fifty percent demon by weight at this point. Holding conflicting beliefs is what I do."

She's cute when she laughs. I pull her on top of me, cupping her sandy butt in my hands as she squirms on top of me, a little sweaty from the sun and quite gritty from the sand. She looks down at me, her hair forming a golden halo shield around our heads.

"I think Bryn might hate me; what am I even going to be going back to?"

"Bryn does not hate you. You got him close enough to lick that sacred nugget of meat and he's going to love you forever for that."

"Nugget of meat!" She laughs. "Have you ever taken anything seriously?"

She asks a lot of questions. I like her questions. A curious Elise who assumes she doesn't have all the answers is preferable to her previous attitude where she thought she knew everything. She's changed a lot, and so have I. Or maybe not. Time will tell.

"I take you seriously. I take killing demons, when they're not one of the many, many demons we're now allied with, seriously. I take our future seriously."

I feel her melt against me. Sometimes she needs reminding in words how much I adore her, how much my world has revolved around her from the moment we met, how I could never, ever be without her.

She kisses me sweetly, and then deeply as I wrap my arms around her and hold her close. She is all that matters in this world or the next, my angel, my lover, my wife.

SMACK!

"Ow!" She complains against my mouth. "What was that for?"

"Anything and everything, forever and ever…"

She giggles, picking up on my cue and kisses me again, wriggling her ass for another one of those smacks she needs, craves, and oh-so-badly deserves before moaning a final coherent word in my ear before we devolve into being nothing more than two grinding, oily beasts knotting on the beach.

"Amen."